Mr. Jack Hamlin's Mediation and Other Stories

Bret Harte

Contents

MR. JACK HAMLIN'S MEDIATION AND OTHER STORIES

BY

Bret Harte

MR. JACK HAMLIN'S MEDIATION

At nightfall it began to rain. The wind arose too, and also began to buffet a small, struggling, nondescript figure, creeping along the trail over the rocky upland meadow towards Rylands's rancho. At times its head was hidden in what appeared to be wings thrown upward from its shoulders; at times its broad-brimmed hat was cocked jauntily on one side, and again the brim was fixed over the face like a visor. At one moment a drifting misshapen mass of drapery, at the next its vague garments, beaten back hard against the figure, revealed outlines far too delicate for that rude enwrapping. For it was Mrs. Rylands herself, in her husband's hat and her "hired man's" old blue army overcoat, returning from the post-office two miles away. The wind continued its aggression until she reached the front door of her newly plastered farmhouse, and then a heavier blast shook the pines above the low-pitched, shingled roof, and sent a shower of arrowy drops after her like a Parthian parting, as she entered. She threw aside the overcoat and hat, and somewhat inconsistently entered the sitting-room, to walk to the window and look back upon the path she had just traversed. The wind and the rain swept down a slope, half meadow, half clearing,--a mile away,--to a fringe of sycamores. A mile further lay the stage road, where, three hours later, her husband would alight on his return from Sacramento. It would be a long wet walk for Joshua Rylands, as their only horse had been borrowed by a neighbor.

In that fading light Mrs. Rylands's oval cheek was shining still from the rain-drops, but there was something in the expression of her worried face that might have as readily suggested tears. She was strikingly handsome, yet quite as incongruous an ornament to her surroundings as she had been to her outer wrappings a moment ago. Even the clothes she now stood in hinted an inadaptibility to the weather--the house--the position she occupied in it. A figured silk dress, spoiled rather than overworn, was still of a quality inconsistent with her evident habits, and the lace-edged petticoat that peeped beneath it was draggled with mud and un-accustomed usage. Her glossy black hair, which had been tossed into curls in some foreign fashion, was now wind-blown into a burlesque of it. This incongruity was still further accented by the appearance of the room she had entered. It was coldly and severely furnished, making the chill of the yet damp white plaster unpleasantly obvious. A black harmonium organ stood in one corner, set out with black and white hymn-books; a trestle-like table contained a large Bible; half a dozen black, horsehair-cushioned chairs stood, geometrically distant, against the walls, from which hung four engravings of "Paradise Lost" in black mourning frames; some dried ferns and autumn leaves stood in a vase on the mantelpiece, as if the chill of the room had prematurely blighted them. The coldly glittering grate below was also decorated with withered sprays, as if an attempt had been made to burn them, but was frustrated through damp. Suddenly recalled to a sense of her wet boots and the new carpet, she hurriedly turned away, crossed the hall into the dining-room, and thence passed into the kitchen. The "hired girl," a large-boned Missourian, a daughter of a neighboring woodman, was peeling potatoes at the table. Mrs. Rylands drew a chair before the kitchen stove, and put her wet feet on the hob.

"I'll bet a cooky, Mess Rylands, you've done forgot the vanillar," said the girl, with a certain domestic and confidential familiarity.

Mrs. Rylands started guiltily. She made a miserable feint of looking in her lap and on the table. "I'm afraid I did, Jane, if I didn't bring it in HERE."

"That you didn't," returned Jane. "And I reckon ye forgot that 'ar pepper-sauce for yer husband."

Mrs. Rylands looked up with piteous contrition. "I really don't know what's the matter with me. I certainly went into the shop, and had it on my list,--and--really"--

Jane evidently knew her mistress, and smiled with superior toleration. "It's kinder bewilderin' goin' in them big shops, and lookin' round them stuffed shelves." The shop at the cross roads and post-office was 14 x 14, but Jane was nurtured on the plains. "Anyhow," she added good-humoredly, "the expressman is sure to look in as he goes by, and you've time to give him the order."

"But is he SURE to come?" asked Mrs. Rylands anxiously. "Mr. Rylands will be so put out without his pepper-sauce."

"He's sure to come ef he knows you're here. Ye kin always kalkilate on that."

"Why?" said Mrs. Rylands abstractedly.

"Why? 'cause he just can't keep his eyes off ye! That's why he comes every day,--'tain't jest for trade!"

This was quite true, not only of the expressman, but of the butcher and baker, and the "candlestick-maker," had there been so advanced a vocation at the cross roads. All were equally and curiously attracted by her picturesque novelty. Mrs. Rylands knew this herself, but without vanity or coquettishness. Possibly that was why the other woman told her. She only slightly deepened the lines of discontent in her cheek and said abstractedly, "Well, when he comes, YOU ask him."

She dried her shoes, put on a pair of slippers that had a faded splendor about them, and went up to her bedroom. Here she hesitated for some time between the sewing-machine and her knitting-needles, but finally settled upon the latter, and a pair of socks for her husband which she had begun a year ago. But she presently despaired of finishing them before he returned, three hours hence, and so applied herself to the sewing-machine. For a little while its singing hum was heard between the blasts that shook the house, but the thread presently snapped, and the machine was put aside somewhat impatiently, with a discontented drawing of the lines around her handsome mouth. Then she began to "tidy" the room, putting a great many things away and bringing out a great many more, a process that was necessarily slow, owing to her falling into attitudes of minute inspection of certain articles of dress, with intervals of trying them on, and observing their effect in her mirror. This kind of interruption also occurred while she was putting away some books that were lying about on chairs and tables, stopping midway to open their pages, becoming interested, and quite finishing one chapter, with the book held close against the window to catch the fading light of day. The feminine reader will gather from this that Mrs. Rylands, though charming, was not facile in domestic duties. She had just glanced at the clock, and lit the candle to again set herself to work, and thus bridge over the two hours more of waiting, when there came a tap at the door. She opened it to Jane.

"There's an entire stranger downstairs, ez hez got a lame hoss and wants to borry a fresh one."

"We have none, you know," said Mrs. Rylands, a little impatiently.

"Thet's what I told him. Then he wanted to know ef he could lie by here till he could get one or fix up his own hoss."

"As you like; you know if you can manage it," said Mrs. Rylands, a little uneasily. "When Mr. Rylands comes you can arrange it between you. Where is he now?"

"In the kitchen."

"The kitchen!" echoed Mrs. Rylands.

"Yes, ma'am, I showed him into the parlor, but he kinder shivered his shoulders, and reckoned ez how he'd go inter the kitchen. Ye see, ma'am, he was all wet, and his shiny big boots was sloppy. But he ain't one o' the stuck-up kind, and he's willin' to make hisself cowf'ble before the kitchen stove."

"Well, then, he don't want ME," said Mrs. Rylands, with a relieved voice.

"Yes'm," said Jane, apparently equally relieved. "Only, I thought I'd just tell you."

A few minutes later, in crossing the upper hall, Mrs. Rylands heard Jane's voice from the kitchen raised in rustic laughter. Had she been satirically inclined, she might have understood Jane's willingness to relieve her mistress of the duty of entertaining the stranger; had she been philosophical, she might have considered the girl's dreary, monotonous life at the rancho, and made allowance for her joy at this rare interruption of it. But I fear that Mrs. Rylands was neither satirical nor philosophical, and presently, when Jane reentered, with color in her alkaline face, and light in her huckleberry eyes, and said she was going over to the cattle-sheds in the "far pasture," to see if the hired man didn't know of some horse that could be got for the stranger, Mrs. Rylands felt a little bitterness in the thought that the girl would have scarcely volunteered to go all that distance in the rain for HER. Yet, in a few moments she forgot all about it, and even the presence of her guest in the house, and in one of her fitful abstracted employments passed through the dining-room into the kitchen, and had opened the door with an "Oh, Jane!" before she remembered her absence.

The kitchen, lit by a single candle, could be only partly seen by her as she stood with her hand on the lock, although she herself was plainly visible. There was a pause, and then a quiet, self-possessed, yet amused, voice answered:--

"My name isn't Jane, and if you're the lady of the house, I reckon yours wasn't

ALWAYS Rylands."

At the sound of the voice Mrs. Rylands threw the door wide open, and as her eyes fell upon the speaker--her unknown guest--she recoiled with a little cry, and a white, startled face. Yet the stranger was young and handsome, dressed with a scrupulousness and elegance which even the stress of travel had not deranged, and he was looking at her with a smile of recognition, mingled with that careless audacity and self-possession which seemed to be the characteristic of his face.

"Jack Hamlin!" she gasped.

"That's me, all the time," he responded easily, "and YOU'RE Nell Montgomery!"

"How did you know I was here? Who told you?" she said impetuously.

"Nobody! never was so surprised in my life! When you opened that door just now you might have knocked me down with a feather." Yet he spoke lazily, with an amused face, and looked at her without changing his position.

"But you MUST have known SOMETHING! It was no mere accident," she went on vehemently, glancing around the room.

"That's where you slip up, Nell," said Hamlin imperturbably. "It WAS an accident and a bad one. My horse lamed himself coming down the grade. I sighted the nearest shanty, where I thought I might get another horse. It happened to be this." For the first time he changed his attitude, and leaned back contemplatively in his chair.

She came towards him quickly. "You didn't use to lie, Jack," she said hesitatingly.

"Couldn't afford it in my business,--and can't now," said Jack cheerfully. "But," he added curiously, as if recognizing something in his companion's agitation, and lifting his brown lashes to her, the window, and the ceiling, "what's all this about? What's your little game here?"

"I'm married," she said, with nervous intensity,--"married, and this is my husband's house!"

"Not married straight out!--regularly fixed?"

"Yes," she said hurriedly.

"One of the boys? Don't remember any Rylands. SPELTER used to be very sweet on you,--but Spelter mightn't have been his real name?"

"None of our lot! No one you ever knew; a--a straight out, square man," she said quickly.

"I say, Nell, look here! You ought to have shown up your cards without even a call. You ought to have told him that you danced at the Casino."

"I did."

"Before he asked you to marry him?"

"Before."

Jack got up from his chair, put his hands in his pockets, and looked at her curiously. This Nell Montgomery, this music-hall "dance and song girl," this girl of whom so much had been SAID and so little PROVED! Well, this was becoming interesting.

"You don't understand," she said, with nervous feverishness; "you remember after that row I had with Jim, that night the manager gave us a supper,--when he treated me like a dog?"

"He did that," interrupted Jack.

"I felt fit for anything," she said, with a half-hysterical laugh, that seemed voiced, however, to check some slumbering memory. "I'd have cut my throat or his, it didn't matter which"--

"It mattered something to us, Nell," put in Jack again, with polite parenthesis; "don't leave US out in the cold."

"I started from 'Frisco that night on the boat ready to fling myself into anything--or the river!" she went on hurriedly. "There was a man in the cabin who noticed me, and began to hang around. I thought he knew who I was,--had seen me on the posters; and as I didn't feel like foolin', I told him so. But he wasn't that kind. He said he saw I was in trouble and wanted me to tell him all."

Mr. Hamlin regarded her cheerfully. "And you told him," he said, "how you had once run away from your childhood's happy home to go on the stage! How you always regretted it, and would have gone back but that the doors were shut forever against you! How you longed to leave, but the wicked men and women around you always"--

"I didn't!" she burst out, with sudden passion; "you know I didn't. I told him everything: who I was, what I had done, what I expected to do again. I pointed out the men--who were sitting there, whispering and grinning at us, as if they were in the front row of the theatre--and said I knew them all, and they knew me. I never spared myself a thing. I said what people said of me, and didn't even care to say it wasn't true!"

"Oh, come!" protested Jack, in perfunctory politeness.

"He said he liked me for telling the truth, and not being ashamed to do it! He said the sin was in the false shame and the hypocrisy; for that's the sort of man he is, you see, and that's like him always! He asked if I would marry him--out of hand--and do my best to be his lawful wife. He said he wanted me to think it over and sleep on it, and to-morrow he would come and see me for an answer. I slipped off the boat at 'Frisco, and went alone to a hotel where I wasn't known. In the morning I didn't know whether he'd keep his word or I'd keep mine. But he came! He said he'd marry me that very day, and take me to his farm in Santa Clara. I agreed. I thought it would take me out of everybody's knowledge, and they'd think me dead! We were married that day, before a regular clergyman. I was married under my own name,"--she stopped and looked at Jack, with a hysterical laugh,--"but he made me write underneath it, 'known as Nell Montgomery;' for he said HE wasn't ashamed of it, nor should I be."

"Does he wear long hair and stick straws in it?" said Hamlin gravely. "Does he 'hear voices' and have 'visions'?"

"He's a shrewd, sensible, hard-working man,--no more mad than you are, nor as mad as I was the day I married him. He's lived up to everything he's said." She stopped, hesitated in her quick, nervous speech; her lip quivered slightly, but she recalled herself, and looking imploringly, yet hopelessly, at Jack, gasped, "And that's what's the matter!"

Jack fixed his eyes keenly upon her. "And you?" he said curtly.

"I?" she repeated wonderingly.

"Yes, what have YOU done?" he said, with sudden sharpness.

The wonder was so apparent in her eyes that his keen glance softened. "Why," she said bewilderingly, "I have been his dog, his slave,--as far as he would let me. I have done everything; I have not been out of the house until he almost drove me out. I have never wanted to go anywhere or see any one; but he has always insisted upon it. I would have been willing to slave here, day and night, and have been happy. But he said I must not seem to be ashamed of my past, when he is not. I would have worn common homespun clothes and calico frocks, and been glad of it, but he insists upon my wearing my best things, even my theatre things; and as he can't afford to buy more, I wear these things I had. I know they look beastly here, and that I'm a laughing-stock, and when I go out I wear almost anything to try and hide them; but," her lip quivered dangerously again, "he wants me to do it, and it pleases him."

Jack looked down. After a pause he lifted his lashes towards her draggled skirt, and said in an easier, conversational tone, "Yes! I thought I knew that dress. I gave it to you for that walking scene in 'High Life,' didn't I?"

"No," she said quickly, "it was the blue one with silver trimming,--don't you remember? I tried to turn it the first year I was married, but it never looked the same."

"It was sweetly pretty," said Jack encouragingly, "and with that blue hat lined with silver, it was just fetching! Somehow I don't quite remember this one," and he looked at it critically.

"I had it at the races in '58, and that supper Judge Boompointer gave us at 'Frisco where Colonel Fish upset the table trying to get at Jim. Do you know," she said, with a little laugh, "it's got the stains of the champagne on it yet; it never would come off. See!" and she held the candle with great animation to the breadth of silk before her.

"And there's more of it on the sleeve," said Jack; "isn't there?"

Mrs. Rylands looked reproachfully at Jack.

"That isn't champagne; don't you know what it is?"

"No!"

"It's blood," she said gravely; "when that Mexican cut poor Ned so bad,--don't you remember? I held his head upon my arm while you bandaged him." She heaved a little sigh, and then added, with a faint laugh, "That's the worst thing about the clothes of a girl in the profession, they get spoiled or stained before they wear out."

This large truth did not seem to impress Mr. Hamlin. "Why did you leave Santa Clara?" he said abruptly, in his previous critical tone.

"Because of the folks there. They were standoffish and ugly. You see, Josh"--

"Who?"

"Josh Rylands!--HIM! He told everybody who I was, even those who had never seen me in the bills,--how good I was to marry him, how he had faith in me and wasn't ashamed,--until they didn't believe we were married at all. So they looked another way when they met us, and didn't call. And all the while I was glad they didn't, but he wouldn't believe it, and allowed I was pining on account of it."

"And were you?"

"I swear to God, Jack, I'd have been content, and more, to have been just there with him, seein' nobody, letting every one believe I was dead and gone, but he said it was wrong, and weak! Maybe it was," she added, with a shy, interrogating look at Jack, of which, however, he took no notice. "Then when he found they wouldn't call, what do you think he did?"

"Beat you, perhaps," suggested Jack cheerfully.

"He never did a thing to me that wasn't straight out, square, and kind," she said, half indignantly, half hopelessly. "He thought if HIS kind of people wouldn't see me, I might like to see my own sort. So without saying anything to me, he brought down, of all things! Tinkie Clifford, she that used to dance in the cheap variety shows at 'Frisco, and her particular friend, Captain Sykes. It would have just killed you, Jack," she said, with a sudden hysteric burst of laughter, "to have seen Josh, in his square, straight-out way, trying to be civil and help things along. But," she went on, as suddenly relapsing into her former attitude of worried appeal, "I couldn't stand it, and when she got to talking free and easy before Josh, and Captain Sykes to guzzling champagne, she and me had a row. She allowed I was putting on airs, and I made her walk, in spite of Josh."

"And Josh seemed to like it," said Hamlin carelessly. "Has he seen her since?"

"No; I reckon he's cured of asking that kind of company for me. And then we came here. But I persuaded him not to begin by going round telling people who I was,--as he did the last time,--but to leave it to folks to find out if they wanted to, and he gave in. Then he let me fix up this house and furnish it my own way, and I did!"

"Do you mean to say that YOU fixed up that family vault of a sitting-room?" said Jack, in horror.

"Yes, I didn't want any fancy furniture or looking-glasses, and such like, to attract folks, nor anything to look like the old times. I don't think any of the boys would care to come here. And I got rid of a lot of sporting travelers, 'wild-cat' managers, and that kind of tramp in this way. But"--She hesitated, and her face fell again.

"But what?" said Jack.

"I don't think that Josh likes it either. He brought home the other day 'My Johnny is a Shoemakiyure,' and wanted me to try it on the organ. But it reminded me how we used to get just sick of singing it on and off the boards, and I couldn't touch it. He wanted me to go to the circus that was touring over at the cross roads, but it was the old Flanigin's circus, you know, the one Gussie Riggs used to ride in, with its old clown and its old ringmaster and the old 'wheezes,' and I chucked it."

"Look here," said Jack, rising and surveying Mrs. Rylands critically. "If you go on at this gait, I'll tell you what that man of yours will do. He'll bolt with some of your old friends!"

She turned a quick, scared face upon him for an instant. But only for an instant. Her hysteric little laugh returned, at once, followed by her weary, worried look. "No, Jack, you don't know him! If it was only that! He cares only for me in his own way,--and," she stammered as she went on, "I've no luck in making him happy."

She stopped. The wind shook the house and fired a volley of rain against the windows. She took advantage of it to draw a torn lace-edged handkerchief from her pocket behind, and keeping the tail of her eyes in a frightened fashion on Jack, applied the handkerchief furtively, first to her nose, and then to her eyes.

"Don't do that," said Jack fastidiously, "it's wet enough outside." Nevertheless, he stood up and gazed at her.

"Well," he began.

She timidly drew nearer to him, and took a seat on the kitchen table, looking up wistfully into his eyes.

"Well," resumed Jack argumentatively, "if he won't 'chuck' you, why don't you 'chuck' HIM?"

She turned quite white, and suddenly dropped her eyes. "Yes," she said, almost inaudibly, "lots of girls would do that."

"I don't mean go back to your old life," continued Jack. "I reckon you've had enough of that. But get into some business, you know, like other women. A bonnet shop, or a candy shop for children, see? I'll help start you. I've got a couple of hundred, if not in my own pocket in somebody's else, just burning to be used! And then you can look about you; and perhaps some square business man will turn up and you can marry him. You know you can't live this way, nohow. It's killing you; it ain't fair on you, nor on Rylands either."

"No," she said quickly, "it ain't fair on HIM. I know it, I know it isn't, I know it isn't," she repeated, "only"--She stopped.

"Only what?" said Jack impatiently.

She did not speak. After a pause she picked up the rolling-pin from the table and began absently rolling it down her lap to her knee, as if pressing out the stained silk skirt. "Only," she stammered, slowly rolling the pin handles in her open palms, "I--I can't leave Josh."

"Why can't you?" said Jack quickly.

"Because--because--I," she went on, with a quivering lip, working the rolling-pin heavily down her knee as if she were crushing her answer out of it,--"because--I--love him!"

There was a pause, a dash of rain against the window, and another dash from her eyes upon her hands, the rolling-pin, and the skirts she had gathered up hastily, as she cried, "O Jack! Jack! I never loved anybody like him! I never knew what love was! I never knew a man like him before! There never WAS one before!"

To this large, comprehensive, and passionate statement Mr. Jack Hamlin made no reply. An audacity so supreme had conquered his. He walked to the window, looked out upon the dark, rain-filmed pane that, however, reflected no equal change in his own dark eyes, and then returned and walked round the kitchen table. When he was at her back, without looking at her, he reached out his hand, took her passive one that lay on the table in his, grasped it heartily for a single moment, laid it gently down, and returned around the table, where he again confronted her cheerfully face to face.

"You'll make the riffle yet," he said quietly. "Just now I don't see what I could do, or where I could chip in your little game; but if I DO, or you do, count me in and let me know. You know where to write,--my old address at Sacramento." He walked to the corner, took up his still wet serape, threw it over his shoulders, and picked up his broad-brimmed riding-hat.

"You're not going, Jack?" she said hesitatingly, as she rubbed her wet eyes into a consciousness of his movements. "You'll wait to see HIM? He'll be here in an hour."

"I've been here too long already," said Jack. "And the less you say about my calling, even accidentally, the better. Nobody will believe it,--YOU didn't yourself. In fact, unless you see how I can help you, the sooner you consider us all dead and buried, the sooner your luck will change. Tell your girl I've found my own horse so much better that I have pushed on with him, and give her that."

He threw a gold coin on the table.

"But your horse is still lame," she said wonderingly. "What will you do in this storm?"

"Get into the cover of the next wood and camp out. I've done it before."

"But, Jack!"

He suddenly made a slight gesture of warning. His quick ear had caught the approach of footsteps along the wet gravel outside. A mischievous light slid into his dark eyes as he coolly moved backward to the door and, holding it open, said, in a remarkably clear and distinct voice:--

"Yes, as you say, society is becoming very mixed and frivolous everywhere, and you'd scarcely know San Francisco now. So delighted, however, to have made your acquaintance, and regret my business prevents my waiting to see your good husband. So odd that I should have known your Aunt Jemima! But, as you say, the world is very small, after all. I shall tell the deacon how well you are looking,--in spite of the kitchen smoke in your eyes. Good-by! A thousand thanks for your hospitality."

And Jack, bowing profoundly to the ground, backed out upon Jane, the hired man, and the expressman, treading, I grieve to say, with some deliberation upon the toes of the two latter, in order, possibly, that in their momentary pain and discomposure they might not scan too closely the face of this ingenious gentleman, as he melted into the night and the storm.

Jane entered, with a slight toss of her head.

"Here's your expressman,--ef you're wantin' him NOW."

Mrs. Rylands was too preoccupied to notice her handmaiden's significant emphasis, as she indicated a fresh-looking, bashful young fellow, whose confusion was evidently heightened by the unexpected egress of Mr. Hamlin, and the point-blank presence of the handsome Mrs. Rylands.

"Oh, certainly," said Mrs. Rylands quickly. "So kind of him to oblige us. Give him the order, Jane, please."

She turned to escape from the kitchen and these new intruders, when her eye fell upon the coin left by Mr. Hamlin. "The gentleman wished you to take that for your trouble, Jane," she said hastily, pointing to it, and passed out.

Jane cast a withering look after her retreating skirts, and picking the coin from the table, turned to the hired man. "Run to the stable after that dandified young feller, Dick, and hand that back to him. Ye kin say that Jane Mackinnon don't run arrants fur money, nor play gooseberry to other folks fur fun."

PART II

Mr. Joshua Rylands had, according to the vocabulary of his class, "found grace" at the age of sixteen, while still in the spiritual state of "original sin" and the political one of Missouri. He had not indeed found it by persistent youthful seeking or spiritual insight, but somewhat violently and turbulently at a camp-meeting. A village boy, naturally gentle and impressible, with an original character,--limited, however, in education and experience,--he had, after his first rustic debauch with some vulgar companions, fallen upon the camp-meeting in reckless audacity; and instead of being handed over to the district constable, was taken in and placed upon "the anxious bench," "rastled with," and exhorted by a strong revivalist preacher, "convicted of sin," and--converted! It is doubtful if the shame of a public arrest and legal punishment would have impressed his youthful spirit as much as did this spiritual examination and trial, in which he himself became accuser. Howbeit, its effect, though punitive, was also exemplary. He at once cast off his evil companions; remaining faithful to his conversion, in spite of their later "backslidings." When, after the Western fashion, the time came for him to forsake his father's farm and seek a new "quarter section" on some more remote frontier, he carried into that secluded, lonely, half-monkish celibacy of pioneer life--which has been the foundation of so much strong Western character--more than the usual religious feeling. At once industrious and adventurous, he lived by "the Word," as he called it, and Nature as he knew it,--tempted by none of the vices or sentiments of civilization. When he finally joined the Californian emigration, it was not as a gold-seeker, but as a discoverer of new agricultural fields; if the hardship was as great and the rewards fewer, he nevertheless knew that he retained his safer isolation and independence of spirit. Vice and civilization were to him synonymous terms; it was the natural condition of the worldly and unregenerate. Such was the man who chanced to meet "Nell Montgomery, the Pearl of the Variety Stage," on the Sacramento boat, in one of his forced visits to civilization. Without knowing her in her profession, her frank exposition of herself did not startle him; he recognized it, accepted it, and strove to convert it. And as long as this daughter of Folly forsook her evil ways for him, it was a triumph in which there was no shame, and might be proclaimed from the housetop. When his neighbors thought differently, and avoided them, he saw no inconsistency in bringing his wife's old friends to divert her: she might in time convert THEM. He had no more fear of her returning to their ways than he had of himself "backsliding." Narrow as was his creed, he had none of the harshness nor pessimism of the bigot. With the keenest self-scrutiny, his credulity regarding others was touching.

The storm was still raging when he alighted that evening from the up coach at the trail nearest his house. Although incumbered with a heavy carpet-bag, he started resignedly on his two-mile tramp without begrudging the neighborly act of his wife which had deprived him of his horse. It was "like her" to do these things in her good-humored abstraction, an abstraction, however, that sometimes worried him, from the fear that it indicated some unhappiness with her present lot. He was longing to rejoin her after his absence of three days, the longest time they had been separated since their marriage, and he hurried on with a certain lover-like excitement, quite new to his usually calm and temperate blood.

Struggling with the storm and darkness, but always with the happy consciousness of drawing nearer to her in that struggle, he labored on, finding his perilous way over the indistinguishable trail by certain landmarks in the distance, visible only to his pioneer eye. That heavier shadow to the right was not the hillside, but the SLOPE to the distant hill; that low, regular line immediately before him was not a fence or wall, but the line of distant gigantic woods, a mile from his home. Yet as he began to descend the slope towards the wood, he stopped and rubbed his eyes.

There was distinctly a light in it. His first idea was that he had lost the trail and was nearing the woodman Mackinnon's cabin. But a more careful scrutiny revealed to him that it was really the wood, and the light was a camp-fire. It was a rough night for camping out, but they were probably some belated prospectors.

When he had reached the fringe of woodland, he could see quite plainly that the fire was built beside one of the large pines, and that the little encampment, which looked quite comfortable and secluded from the storm-beaten trail, was occupied apparently by a single figure. By the good glow of the leaping fire, that figure standing erect before it, elegantly shaped, in the graceful folds of a serape, looked singularly romantic and picturesque, and reminded Joshua Rylands--whose ideas of art were purely reminiscent of boyish reading--of some picture in a novel. The heavy black columns of the pines, glancing out of the concave shadow, also seemed a fitting background to what might have been a scene in a play. So strongly was he impressed by it that but for his anxiety to reach his home, still a mile distant, and the fact that he was already late, he would have penetrated the wood and the seclusion of the stranger with an offer of hospitality for the night. The man, however, was evidently capable of taking care of himself, and the outline of a tethered horse was faintly visible under another tree. It might be a surveyor or engineer,--the only men of a better class who were itinerant.

But another and even greater surprise greeted him as he toiled up the rocky slope towards his farmhouse. The windows of the sitting-room, which were usually blank and black by night, were glittering with unfamiliar light. Like most farmers, he seldom used the room except for formal company, his wife usually avoiding it, and even he himself now preferred the dining-room or the kitchen. His first suggestion that his wife had visitors gave him a sense of pleasure on her account, mingled, however, with a slight uneasiness of his own which he could not account for. More than that, as he approached nearer he could hear the swell of the organ above the roar of the swaying pines, and the cadences were not of a devotional character. He hesitated for a moment, as he had hesitated at the fire in the woods; yet it was surely his own house! He hurried to the door, opened it; not only the light of the sitting-room streamed into the hall, but the ruddier glow of an actual fire in the disused grate! The familiar dark furniture had been rearranged to catch some of the glow and relieve its sombreness. And his wife, rising from the music-stool, was the room's only occupant!

Mrs. Rylands gazed anxiously and timidly at her husband's astonished face, as he threw off his waterproof and laid down his carpet-bag. Her own face was a little flurried with excitement, and his, half hidden in his tawny beard, and, possibly owing to his self-introspective nature, never spontaneously sympathetic, still expressed only wonder! Mrs. Rylands was a little frightened. It is sometimes dangerous to meddle with a man's habits, even when he has grown weary of them.

"I thought," she began hesitatingly, "that it would be more cheerful for you in here, this stormy evening. I thought you might like to put your wet things to dry in the kitchen, and we could sit here together, after supper, alone."

I am afraid that Mrs. Rylands did not offer all her thoughts. Ever since Mr. Hamlin's departure she had been uneasy and excited, sometimes falling into fits of dejection, and again lighting up into hysterical levity; at other times carefully examining her wardrobe, and then with a sudden impulse rushing downstairs again to give orders for her husband's supper, and to make the extraordinary changes in the sitting-room already noted. Only a few moments before he arrived, she had covertly brought down a piece of music, and put aside the hymn-books, and taken, with a little laugh, a pack of cards from her pocket, which she placed behind the already dismantled vase on the chimney.

"I reckoned you had company, Ellen," he said gravely, kissing her.

"No," she said quickly. "That is," she stopped with a sudden surge of color in her face that startled her, "there was--a man--here, in the kitchen--who had a lame horse, and who wanted to get a fresh one. But he went away an hour ago. And he wasn't in this room--at least, after it was fixed up. So I've had no company."

She felt herself again blushing at having blushed, and a little terrified. There was no reason for it. But for Jack's warning, she would have been quite ready to tell her husband all. She had never blushed before him over her past life; why she should now blush over seeing Jack, of all people! made her utter a little hysterical laugh. I am afraid that this experienced little woman took it for granted that her husband knew that if Jack or any man had been there as a clandestine lover, she would not have blushed at all. Yet with all her experience, she did not know that she had blushed simply because it was to Jack that she had confessed that she loved the man before her. Her husband noted the blush as part of her general excitement.

He permitted her to drag him into the room and seat him before the hearth, where she sank down on one knee to pull off his heavy rubber boots. But he waved her aside at this, pulled them off with his own hands, and let her take them to the kitchen and bring back his slippers. By this time a smile had lighted up his hard face. The room was certainly more comfortable and cheerful. Still he was a little worried; was there not in these changes a falling away from the grace of self-abnegation which she had so sedulously practiced?

When supper was served by Jane, in the dull dining-room, Mr. Rylands, had he not been more engaged in these late domestic changes, might have noticed that the Missouri girl waited upon him with a certain commiserating air that was remarkable by its contrast with the frigid ceremonious politeness with which she attended her mistress. It had not escaped Mrs. Rylands, however, who ever since Jack's abrupt departure had noticed this change in the girl's demeanor to herself, and with a woman's intuitive insight of another woman, had fathomed it. The comfortable tete-a-tete with Jack, which Jane had looked forward to, Mrs. Rylands had anticipated herself, and then sent him off! When Joshua thanked his wife for remembering the pepper-sauce, and Mrs. Rylands pathetically admitted her forgetfulness, the head-toss which Jane gave as she left the room was too marked to be overlooked by him. Mrs. Rylands gave a hysterical little laugh. "I am afraid Jane doesn't like my sending away the expressman just after I had also dismissed the stranger whom she had taken a fancy to, and left her without company," she said unwisely.

Mr. Rylands did not laugh. "I reckon," he returned slowly, "that Jane must feel kinder lonely; she bears all the burden of our bein' outer the world, without any of our glory in the cause of it."

Nevertheless, when supper was over, and the pair were seated in the sitting-room before the fire, this episode was forgotten. Mrs. Rylands produced her husband's pipe and tobacco-pouch. He looked around the formal walls and hesitated. He had been in the habit of smoking in the kitchen.

"Why not here?" said Mrs. Rylands, with a sudden little note of decision. "Why should we keep this room only for company that don't come? I call it silly."

This struck Mr. Rylands as logical. Besides, undoubtedly the fire had mellowed the room. After a puff or two he looked at his wife musingly. "Couldn't you make yourself one of them cigarettys, as they call 'em? Here's the tobacco, and I'll get you the paper."

"I COULD," she said tentatively. Then suddenly, "What made you think of it? You never saw ME smoke!"

"No," said Rylands, "but that lady, your old friend, Miss Clifford, does, and I thought you might be hankering after it."

"How do you know Tinkie Clifford smokes?" said Mrs. Rylands quickly.

"She lit a cigaretty that day she called."

"I hate it," said Mrs. Rylands shortly.

Mr. Rylands nodded approval, and puffed meditatively.

"Josh, have you seen that girl since?"

"No," said Joshua.

"Nor any other girl like her?"

"No," said Joshua wonderingly. "You see I only got to know her on your account, Ellen, that she might see you."

"Well, don't you do it any more! None of 'em! Promise me!" She leaned forward eagerly in her chair.

"But Ellen,"--her husband began gravely.

"I know what you're going to say, but they can't do me any good, and you can't do them any good as you did ME, so there!"

Mr. Rylands was silent, and smiled meditatively.

"Josh!"

"Yes."

"When you met me that night on the Sacramento boat, and looked at me, did you--did I," she hesitated,--"did you look at me because I had been crying?"

"I thought you were troubled in spirit, and looked so."

"I suppose I looked worried, of course; I had no time to change or even fix my hair; I had on that green dress, and it NEVER was becoming. And you only spoke to me on account of my awful looks?"

"I saw only your wrestling soul, Ellen, and I thought you needed comfort and help."

She was silent for a moment, and then, leaning forward, picked up the poker and began to thrust it absently between the bars.

"And if it had been some other girl crying and looking awful, you'd have spoken to her all the same?"

This was a new idea to Mr. Rylands, but with most men logic is supreme. "I suppose I would," he said slowly.

"And married her?" She rattled the bars of the grate with the poker as if to drown the inevitable reply.

Mr. Rylands loved the woman before him, but it pleased him to think that he loved truth better. "If it had been necessary to her salvation, yes," he said.

"Not Tinkie?" she said suddenly.

"SHE never would have been in your contrite condition."

"Much you know! Girls like that can cry as well as laugh, just as they want to. Well! I suppose I DID look horrid." Nevertheless, she seemed to gain some gratification from her husband's reply, and changed the subject as if fearful of losing that satisfaction by further questioning.

"I tried some of those songs you brought, but I don't think they go well with the harmonium," she said, pointing to some music on its rack, "except one. Just listen." She rose, and with the same nervous quickness she had shown before, went to the instrument and began to sing and play. There was a hopeless incongruity between the character of the instrument and the spirit of the song. Mrs. Rylands's voice was rather forced and crudely trained, but Joshua Rylands, sitting there comfortably slippered by the fire and conscious of the sheeted rain against the window, felt it good. Presently he arose, and lounging heavily over to the fair performer, leaned down and imprinted a kiss on the labyrinthine fringes of her hair. At which Mrs. Rylands caught blindly at his hand nearest her, and without lifting her other hand from the keys, or her eyes from the music, said tentatively:--

"You know there's a chorus just here! Why can't you try it with me?"

Mr. Rylands hesitated a moment, then, with a preliminary cough, lifted a voice as crude as hers, but powerful through much camp-meeting exercise, and roared a chorus which was remarkable chiefly for requiring that archness and playfulness in execution which he lacked. As the whole house seemed to dilate with the sound, and the wind outside to withhold its fury, Mr. Rylands felt that physical delight which children feel in personal outcry, and was grateful to his wife for the opportunity. Laying his hand affectionately on her shoulder, he noticed for the first time that she was in a kind of evening-dress, and that her delicate white shoulder shone through the black lace that enveloped it.

For an instant Mr. Rylands was shocked at this unwonted exposure. He had never seen his wife in evening-dress before. It was true they were alone, and in their own sitting-room, but the room was still invested with that formality and publicity which seemed to accent this indiscretion. The simple-minded frontier man's mind went back to Jane, to the hired man, to the expressman, the stranger, all of whom might have noticed it also.

"You have a new dress," he said slowly, "have you worn it all day?"

"No," she said, with a timid smile. "I only put it on just before you came. It's the one I used to wear in the ballroom scene in 'Gay Times in 'Frisco.' You don't know it, I know. I thought I would wear it tonight, and then," she suddenly grasped his hand, "you'll let me put all these things away forever! Won't you, Josh? I've seen such nice pretty calico at the store to-day, and I can make up one or two home dresses, like Jane's, only better fitting, of course. In fact, I asked them to send the roll up here to-morrow for you to see."

Mr. Rylands felt relieved. Perhaps his views had changed about the moral effect of her retaining these symbols of her past, for he consented to the calico dresses, not, however, without an inward suspicion that she would not look so well in them, and that the one she had on was more becoming.

Meantime she tried another piece of music. It was equally incongruous and slightly Bacchantic.

"There used to be a mighty pretty dance went to that," she said, nodding her head in time with the music, and assisting the heavily spasmodic attempts of the instrument with the pleasant levity of her voice. "I used to do it."

"Ye might try it now, Ellen," suggested her husband, with a half-frightened, half-amused tolerance.

"YOU play, then," said Mrs. Rylands quickly, offering her seat to him.

Mr. Rylands sat down to the harmonium, as Mrs. Rylands briskly moved the table and chairs against the wall. Mr. Rylands played slowly and strenuously, as from a conscientious regard of the instrument. Mrs. Rylands stood in the centre of the floor, making a rather pretty, animated picture, as she again stimulated the heavy harmonium swell not only with her voice but her hands and feet. Presently she began to skip.

I should warn the reader here that this was before the "shawl" or "skirt" dancing was in vogue, and I am afraid that pretty Mrs. Rylands's performances would now be voted slow. Her silk skirt and frilled petticoat were lifted just over her small ankles and tiny bronze-kid shoes. In the course of a pirouette or two, there was a slight further revelation of blue silk stockings and some delicate embroidery, but really nothing more than may be seen in the sweep of a modern waltz. Suddenly the music ceased. Mr. Rylands had left the harmonium and walked over to the hearth. Mrs. Rylands stopped, and came towards him with a flushed, anxious face.

"It don't seem to go right, does it?" she said, with her nervous laugh. "I suppose I'm getting too old now, and I don't quite remember it."

"Better forget it altogether," he replied gravely. He stopped at seeing a singular change in her face, and added awkwardly, "When I told you I didn't want you to be ashamed of your past, nor to try to forget what you were, I didn't mean such things as that!"

"What did you mean?" she said timidly.

The truth was that Mr. Rylands did not know. He had known this sort of thing only in the abstract. He had never had the least acquaintance with the class to which his wife had belonged, nor known anything of their methods. It was a revelation to him now, in the woman he loved, and who was his wife. He was not shocked so much as he was frightened.

"You shall have the dress to-morrow, Ellen," he said gently, "and you can put away these gewgaws. You don't need to look like Tinkie Clifford."

He did not see the look of triumph that lit up her eye, but added, "Go on and play."

She sat down obediently to the instrument. He watched her for a few moments from the toe of her kid slipper on the pedals to the swell of her shoulders above the keyboard, with a strange, abstracted face. Presently she stopped and came over to him.

"And when I've got these nice calico frocks, and you can't tell me from Jane, and I'm a good housekeeper, and settle down to be a farmer's wife, maybe I'll have a secret to tell you."

"A secret?" he repeated gravely. "Why not now?"

Her face was quite aglow with excitement and a certain timid mischief as she laughed: "Not while you are so solemn. It can wait."

He looked at his watch. "I must give some orders to Jim about the stock before he turns in," he said.

"He's gone to the stables already," said Mrs. Rylands.

"No matter; I can go there and find him."

"Shall I bring your boots?" she said quickly.

"I'll put them on when I pass through the kitchen. I won't be long away. Now go to bed. You are looking tired," he said gently, as he gazed at the drawn lines about her eyes and mouth. Her former pretty color struck him also as having changed of late, and as being irregular and inharmonious.

As Mrs. Rylands obediently ascended the stairs she heaved a faint sigh, her only recognition of her husband's criticism. He turned and passed quickly into the kitchen. He wanted to be alone to collect his thoughts. But he was surprised to find Jane still there, sitting bolt upright in a chair in the corner. Apparently she had been expecting him, for as he entered she stood up, and wiped her cheek and mouth with one hand, as if to compress her lips the more tightly.

"I reckoned," she began, "that unless you war for forgettin' everythin' in these yer goings on, ye'd be passin' through here to tend to your stock. I've got a word to say to ye, Mr. Rylands. When I first kem over here to help, I got word from the folks around that your wife afore you married her was just one o' them bally dancers. Well, that was YOUR lookout, not mine! Jane Mackinnon ain't the kind to take everybody's sayin' as gospil, but she kalkilates to treat folks ez she finds 'em. When she finds 'em lyin' and deceivin'; when she finds em purtendin' one thing and doin' another; when she finds 'em makin' fools tumble to 'em; playing soots on their own husbands, and turnin' an honest house into a music-hall and a fandango shop, she kicks! You hear me! Jane Mackinnon kicks!"

"What do you mean?" said Mr. Rylands sternly.

"I mean," said Miss Mackinnon, striking her hips with the back of her hands smartly, and accenting each word that dropped like a bullet from her mouth with an additional blow,--"I--mean--that--your--wife--had one--of--her--old--hangers-on--from--'Frisco--here--in--this very--kitchen--all--the--arternoon; there! I mean that whiles she was waitin' here for you, she was canoodlin' and cryin' over old times with him! I saw her myself through the winder. That's what I mean, Mr.

Joshua Rylands."

"It's false! She had some poor stranger here with a lame horse. She told me so herself."

Jane Mackinnon laughed shrilly.

"Did she tell you that the poor stranger was young and pretty-faced, with black moustarches? that his store clothes must have cost a fortin, saying nothing of his gold-lined, broadcloth sarrapper? Did she say that his horse was so lame that when I went to get another he wouldn't WAIT for it? Did she tell you WHO he was?"

"No, she did not know," said Rylands sternly, but with a whitening face.

"Well, I'll tell you! The gambler, the shooter!--the man whose name is black enough to stain any woman he knows. Jim recognized him like a shot; he sez, the moment he clapped eyes on him at the door, 'Dod blasted, if it ain't Jack Hamlin!'"

Little as Mr. Rylands knew of the world, he had heard that name. But it was not THAT he was thinking of. He was thinking of the camp-fire in the wood, the handsome figure before it, the tethered horse. He was thinking of the lighted sitting-room, the fire, his wife's bare shoulders, her slippers, stockings, and the dance. He saw it all,--a lightning-flash to his dull imagination. The room seemed to expand and then grow smaller, the figure of Jane to sway backwards and forwards before him. He murmured the name of God with lips that were voiceless, caught at the kitchen table to steady himself, held it till he felt his arms grow rigid, and then recovered himself,--white, cold, and sane.

"Speak a word of this to HER," he said deliberately, "enter her room while I'm gone, even leave the kitchen before I come back, and I'll throw you into the road. Tell that hired man, if he dares to breathe it to a soul I'll strangle him."

The unlooked-for rage of this quiet, God-fearing man, and dupe, as she believed, was terrible, but convincing. She shrank back into the corner as he coolly drew on his boots and waterproof, and without another word left the house.

He knew what he was going to do as well as if it had been ordained for him. He knew he would find the young man in the wood; for whatever were the truth of the other stories, he and the visitor were identical; he had seen him with his own eyes. He would confront him face to face and know all; and until then, he could not see his wife again. He walked on rapidly, but without feverishness or mental confusion. He saw his duty plainly,--if Ellen had "backslidden," he must give her another trial.

These were his articles of faith. He should not put her away; but she should nevermore be wife to him. It was HE who had tempted her, it was true; perhaps God would forgive her for that reason, but HE could never love her again.

The fury of the storm had somewhat abated as he reached the wood. The fire was still there, but no longer a leaping flame. A dull glow in the darkness of the forest aisles was all that indicated its position. Rylands at once plunged in that direction; he was near enough to see the red embers when he heard a sharp click, and a voice called:--

"Hold up!"

Mr. Hamlin was a light sleeper. The crackle of underbrush had been enough to disturb him. The voice was his; the click was the cocking of his revolver.

Rylands was no coward, but halted diplomatically.

"Now, then," said Mr. Hamlin's voice, "a little more this way, IN THE LIGHT, if you please!"

Rylands moved as directed, and saw Mr. Hamlin lying before the fire, resting easily on one hand, with his revolver in the other.

"Thank you!" said Jack. "Excuse my precautions, but it is night, and this is, for the present, my bedroom."

"My name is Rylands; you called at my house this afternoon and saw my wife," said Rylands slowly.

"I did," said Hamlin. "It was mighty kind of you to return my call so soon, but I didn't expect it."

"I reckon not. But I know who you are, and that you are an old associate of hers, in the days of her sin and unregeneration. I want you to answer me, before God and man, what was your purpose in coming there to-day?"

"Look here! I don't think it's necessary to drag in strangers to hear my answer," said Jack, lying down again, "but I came to borrow a horse."

"Is that the truth?"

Jack got upon his feet very solemnly, put on his hat, drew down his waistcoat, and approached Mr. Rylands with his hands in his pockets.

"Mr. Rylands," he said, with great suavity of manner, "this is the second time today that I have had the honor of having my word doubted by your family. Your wife was good enough to question my assertion that I didn't know that she was living here, but that was a woman's vanity. You have no such excuse. There is my horse yonder, lame, as you may see. I didn't lame him for the sake of seeing your wife nor you."

There was that in Mr. Hamlin's audacity and perfect self-possession which, even while it irritated, never suggested deceit. He was too reckless of consequence to lie. Mr. Rylands was staggered and half convinced. Nevertheless, he hesitated.

"Dare you tell me everything that happened between my wife and you?"

"Dare you listen?" said Mr. Hamlin quietly.

Mr. Rylands turned a little white. After a moment he said:--

"Yes."

"Good!" said Mr. Hamlin. "I like your grit, though I don't mind telling you it's the ONLY thing I like about you. Sit down. Well, I haven't seen Nell Montgomery for three years until I met her as your wife, at your house. She was surprised as I was, and frightened as I wasn't. She spent the whole interview in telling me the history of her marriage and her life with you, and nothing more. I cannot say that it was remarkably entertaining, or that she was as amusing as your wife as she was as Nell Montgomery, the variety actress. When she had finished, I came away."

Mr. Rylands, who had seated himself, made a movement as if to rise. But Mr. Hamlin laid his hand on his knee.

"I asked you if you dared to listen. I have something myself to say of that interview. I found your wife wearing the old dresses that other men had given her, and she said she wore them because she thought it pleased you. I found that you, who are questioning my calling upon her, had already got the worst of her old chums to visit her without asking her consent; I found that instead of being the first one to lie for her and hide her, you were the first one to tell anybody her history, just because you thought it was to the glory of God generally, and of Joshua Rylands in particular."

"A man's motives are his own," stammered Rylands.

"Sorry you didn't see it when you questioned mine just now," said Jack coolly.

"Then she complained to you?" said Rylands hesitatingly.

"I didn't say that," said Jack shortly.

"But you found her unhappy?"

"Damnably."

"And you advised her"--said Rylands tentatively.

"I advised her to chuck you and try to get a better husband." He paused, and then added, with a disgusted laugh, "but she didn't tumble to it, for a d----d silly reason."

"What reason?" said Rylands hurriedly.

"Said she LOVED you," returned Jack, kicking a brand back into the fire. Mr. Rylands's white cheeks flamed out suddenly like the brand. Seeing which, Jack turned upon him deliberately.

"Mr. Joshua Rylands, I've seen many fools in my time. I've seen men holding four aces backed down because they thought they KNEW the other man had a royal flush! I've seen a man sell his claim for a wild-cat share, with the gold lying a foot below him in the ground he walked on. I've seen a dead shot shoot wild because he THOUGHT he saw something in the other man's eye. I've seen a heap of God-forsaken fools, but I never saw one before who claimed God as a pal. You've got a wife a d----d sight truer to you for what you call her 'sin,' than you've ever been to her, with all your d----d salvation! And as you couldn't make her otherwise, though you've tried to hard enough, it seems to me that for square downright chuckle-headedness, you can take the cake! Good-night! Now, run away and play! You're making me tired."

"One moment," said Mr. Rylands awkwardly and hurriedly. "I may have wronged you; I was mistaken. Won't you come back with me and accept my--our--hospitality?"

"Not much," said Jack. "I left your house because I thought it better for you and her that no one should know of my being there."

"But you were already recognized," said Mr. Rylands. "It was Jane who lied about you, and your return with me will confute her slanders."

"Who?" asked Jack.

"Jane, our hired girl."

Mr. Hamlin uttered an indescribable laugh.

"That's just as well! You simply tell Jane you SAW me; that I was greatly shocked at what she said, but that I forgive her. I don't think she'll say any more."

Strange to add, Mr. Hamlin's surmise was correct. Mr. Rylands found Jane still in the kitchen alone, terrified, remorseful, yet ever after silent on the subject. Stranger still, the hired man became equally uncommunicative. Mrs. Rylands, attributing her husband's absence only to care of the stock, had gone to bed in a feverish condition, and Mr. Rylands did not deem it prudent to tell her of his interview. The next day she sent for the doctor, and it was deemed necessary for her to keep her bed for a few days. Her husband was singularly attentive and considerate during that time, and it was probable that Mrs. Rylands seized that opportunity to tell him the secret she spoke of the night before. Whatever it was,--for it was not generally known for a few months later,--it seemed to draw them closer together, imparted a protecting dignity to Joshua Rylands, which took the place of his former selfish austerity, gave them a future to talk of confidentially, hopefully, and sometimes foolishly, which took the place of their more foolish past, and when the roll of calico came from the cross roads, it contained also a quantity of fine linen, laces, small caps, and other trifles, somewhat in contrast to the more homely materials ordered.

And when three months were past, the sitting-room was often lit up and made cheerful, particularly on that supreme occasion when, with a great deal of enthusiasm, all the women of the countryside flocked to see Mrs. Rylands and her first baby. And a more considerate and devoted couple than the father and mother they had never known.

THE MAN AT THE SEMAPHORE

In the early days of the Californian immigration, on the extremest point of the sandy peninsula, where the bay of San Francisco debouches into the Pacific, there stood a semaphore telegraph. Tossing its black arms against the sky,-- with its back to the Golden Gate and that vast expanse of sea whose nearest shore was Japan,--it signified to another semaphore further inland the "rigs" of incoming vessels, by certain uncouth signs, which were again passed on to Telegraph Hill, San Francisco, where they reappeared on a third semaphore, and read to the initiated "schooner," "brig" "ship," or "steamer." But all homesick San Francisco had learned the last sign, and on certain days of the month every eye was turned to welcome those gaunt arms widely extended at right angles, which meant "side-wheel steamer" (the only steamer which carried the mails) and "letters from home." In the joyful reception accorded to that herald of glad tidings, very few thought of the lonely watcher on the sand dunes who dispatched them, or even knew of that desolate Station.

For desolate it was beyond description. The Presidio, with its voiceless, dismounted cannon and empty embrasures hidden in a hollow, and the Mission Dolores, with its crumbling walls and belfry tower lost in another, made the ultima thule of all San Francisco wandering. The Cliff house and Fort Point did not then exist; from Black Point the curving line of shore of "Yerba Buena"--or San Francisco--showed only a stretch of glittering wind-swept sand dunes, interspersed with straggling gullies of half-buried black "scrub oak." The long six months' summer sun fiercely beat upon it from the cloudless sky above; the long six months' trade winds fiercely beat upon it from the west; the monotonous roll-call of the long Pacific surges regularly beat upon it from the sea. Almost impossible to face by day through sliding sands and buffeting winds, at night it was impracticable through the dense sea-fog that stole softly through the Golden Gate at sunset. Thence, until morning, sea and shore were a trackless waste, bounded only by the warning thunders of the unseen sea. The station itself, a rudely built cabin, with two windows,--one furnished with a telescope,--looked like a heap of driftwood, or a stranded wreck left by the retiring sea; the semaphore--the only object for leagues--lifted above the undulating dunes, took upon itself various shapes, more or less gloomy, according to the hour or weather,--a blasted tree, the masts and clinging spars of a beached ship, a dismantled gallows; or, with the background of a golden sunset across the Gate, and its arms extended at right angles, to a more hopeful fancy it might have seemed the missionary Cross, which the enthusiast Portala lifted on that heathen shore a hundred years before.

Not that Dick Jarman--the solitary station keeper--ever indulged this fancy. An escaped convict from one of her Britannic Majesty's penal colonies, a "stowaway" in the hold of an Australian ship, he had landed penniless in San Francisco, fearful of contact with his more honest countrymen already there, and liable to detection at any moment. Luckily for him, the English immigration consisted mainly of gold-seekers en route to Sacramento and the southern mines. He was prudent enough to resist the temptation to follow them, and accepted the post of semaphore keeper,--the first work offered him,--which the meanest immigrant, filled with dreams of gold, would have scorned. His employers asked him no questions, and demanded no references; his post could be scarcely deemed one of trust,--there was no property for him to abscond with but the telescope; he was removed from temptation and evil company in his lonely waste; his duties were as mechanical as the instrument he worked, and interruption of them would be instantly known at San Francisco. For this he would receive his board and lodging and seventy-five dollars a month,--a sum to be ridiculed in those "flush days," but which seemed to the broken-spirited and half-famished stowaway a princely independence.

And then there was rest and security! He was free from that torturing anxiety and fear of detection which had haunted him night and day for three months. The ceaseless vigilance and watchful dread he had known since his escape, he could lay aside now. The rude cabin on the sand dune was to him as the long-sought cave to some hunted animal. It seemed impossible that any one would seek him there. He was spared alike the contact of his enemies or the shame of recognizing even a friendly face, until by each he would be forgotten. From his coign of vantage on that desolate waste, and with the aid of his telescope, no stranger could approach within two or three miles of his cabin without undergoing his scrutiny. And at the worst, if he was pursued here, before him was the trackless shore and the boundless sea!

And at times there was a certain satisfaction in watching, unseen and in perfect security, the decks of passing ships. With the aid of his glass he could mingle again with the world from which he was debarred, and gloomily wonder who among those passengers knew their solitary watcher, or had heard of his deeds; it might have made him gloomier had he known that in those eager faces turned towards the golden haven there was little thought of anything but themselves. He tried to read in faces on board the few outgoing ships the record of their success with a strange envy. They were returning home! HOME! For sometimes--but seldom--he thought of his own home and his past. It was a miserable past of forgery and embezzlement that had culminated a career of youthful dissipation and self-indulgence, and shut him out, forever, from the staid old English cathedral town where he was born. He knew that his relations believed and wished him dead. He thought of this past with little pleasure, but with little remorse. Like most of his stamp, he believed it was ill-luck, chance, somebody else's fault, but never his own responsible action. He would not repent; he would be wiser only. And he would not be retaken--alive!

Two or three months passed in this monotonous duty, in which he partly recovered his strength and his nerves. He lost his furtive, restless, watchful look; the bracing sea air and the burning sun put into his face the healthy tan and the up-lifted frankness of a sailor. His eyes grew keener from long scanning of the horizon; he knew where to look for sails, from the creeping coastwise schooner to the far-rounding merchantman from Cape Horn. He knew the faint line of haze that indicated the steamer long before her masts and funnels became visible. He saw no soul except the solitary boatman of the little "plunger," who landed his weekly provisions at a small cove hard by. The boatman thought his secretiveness and reticence only the surliness of his nation, and cared little for a man who never asked for the news, and to whom he brought no letters. The long nights which wrapped the cabin in sea-fog, and at first seemed to heighten the exile's sense of security, by degrees, however, became monotonous, and incited an odd restlessness, which he was wont to oppose by whiskey,--allowed as a part of his stores,--which, while it dulled his sensibilities, he, however, never permitted to interfere with his mechanical duties.

He had been there five months, and the hills on the opposite shore between Tamalpais were already beginning to show their russet yellow sides. One bright morning he was watching the little fleet of Italian fishing-boats hovering in the bay. This was always a picturesque spectacle, perhaps the only one that relieved the general monotony of his outlook. The quaint lateen sails of dull red, or yellow, showing against the sparkling waters, and the red caps or handkerchiefs of the fishermen, might have attracted even a more abstracted man. Suddenly one of the larger boats tacked, and made directly for the little cove where his weekly plunger used to land. In an instant he was alert and suspicious. But a close examination of the boat through his glass satisfied him that it contained, in addition to the crew, only two or three women, apparently the family of the fishermen. As it ran up on the beach and the entire party disembarked he could see it was merely a careless, peaceable invasion, and he thought no more about it. The strangers wandered about the sands, gesticulating and laughing; they brought a pot ashore, built a fire, and cooked a homely meal. He could see that from time to time the semaphore--evidently a novelty to them--had attracted their attention; and having occasion to signal the arrival of a bark, the working of the uncouth arms of the instrument drew the children in half-frightened curiosity towards it, although the others held aloof, as if fearful of trespassing upon some work of the government, no doubt secretly guarded by the police. A few mornings later he was surprised to see upon the beach, near the same locality, a small heap of lumber which had evidently been landed in the early morning fog. The next day an old tent appeared on the spot, and the men, evidently fishermen, began the erection of a rude cabin beside it. Jarman had been long enough there to know that it was government land, and that these manifestly humble "squatters" upon it would not be interfered with for some time to come. He began to be uneasy again; it was true they were fully half a mile from him, and they were foreigners; but might not their reckless invasion of the law attract others, in this lawless country, to do the same? It ought to be stopped. For once Richard Jarman sided with legal authority.

But when the cabin was completed, it was evident from what he saw of its rude structure that it was only a temporary shelter for the fisherman's family and the stores, and refitting of the fishing-boat, more convenient to them than the San Francisco wharves. The beach was utilized for the mending of nets and sails, and thus became half picturesque. In spite of the keen northwestern trades, the cloudless, sunshiny mornings tempted these southerners back to their native al fresco existence; they not only basked in the sun, but many of their household duties, and even the mysteries of their toilet, were performed in the open air. They did not seem to care to penetrate into the desolate region behind them; their half-amphibious habit kept them near the water's edge, and Richard Jarman, after taking his limited walks for the first few mornings in another direction, found it no longer necessary to avoid the locality, and even forgot their propinquity.

But one morning, as the fog was clearing away and the sparkle of the distant sea was beginning to show from his window, he rose from his belated breakfast to fetch water from the "breaker" outside, which had to be replenished weekly from Sancelito, as there was no spring in his vicinity. As he opened the door, he was inexpressibly startled by the figure of a young woman standing in front of it, who, however, half fearfully, half laughingly withdrew before him. But his own manifest disturbance apparently gave her courage.

"I jess was looking at that thing," she said bashfully, pointing to the semaphore.

He was still more astonished, for, looking at her dark eyes and olive complexion, he had expected her to speak Italian or broken English. And, possibly because for a long time he had seen and known little of women, he was quite struck with her good looks. He hesitated, stammered, and then said:--

"Won't you come in?"

She drew back still farther and made a rapid gesture of negation with her head, her hand, and even her whole lithe figure. Then she said, with a decided American intonation:--

"No, sir."

"Why not?" said Jarman mechanically.

The girl sidled up against the cabin, keeping her eyes fixed on Jarman with a certain youthful shrewdness.

"Oh, you know!" she said.

"I really do not. Tell me why."

She drew herself up against the wall a little proudly, though still youthfully, with her hands behind her.

"I ain't that kind of girl," she said simply.

The blood rushed to Jarman's checks. Dissipated and abandoned as his life had been, small respecter of women as he was, he was shocked and shamed. Knowing too, as he did, how absorbed he was in other things, he was indignant, because not guilty.

"Do as you please, then," he said shortly, and reentered the cabin. But the next moment he saw his error in betraying an irritation that was open to misconstruction. He came out again, scarcely looking at the girl, who was lounging away.

"Do you want me to explain to you how the thing works?" he said indifferently. "I can't show you unless a ship comes in."

The girl's eyes brightened softly as she turned to him.

"Do tell me," she said, with an anticipatory smile and flash of white teeth. "Won't you?"

She certainly was very pretty and simple, in spite of her late speech. Jarman briefly explained to her the movements of the semaphore arms and their different significance. She listened with her capped head a little on one side like an attentive bird, and her arms unconsciously imitating the signs. Certainly, for all that she SPOKE like an American, her gesticulation was Italian.

"And then," she said triumphantly when he paused, "when the sailors see that sign up they know they are coming in the harbor."

Jarman smiled, as he had not smiled since he had been there. He corrected this mistake of her eager haste to show her intelligence, and, taking the telescope, pointed out the other semaphore,--a thin black outline on a distant inland hill. He then explained how HIS signs were repeated by that instrument to San Francisco.

"My! Why, I always allowed that was only the cross stuck up in the Lone Mountain Cemetery," she said.

"You are a Catholic?"

"I reckon."

"And you are an Italian?"

"Father is, but mother was a 'Merikan, same as me. Mother's dead."

"And your father is the fisherman yonder?"

"Yes,--but," with a look of pride, "he's got the biggest boat of any."

"And only you and your family are ashore here?"

"Yes, and sometimes Mark." She laughed an odd little laugh.

"Mark? Who's he?" he asked quickly.

He had not noticed the sudden coquettish pose and half-affected bashfulness of the girl; he was thinking only of the possibility of detection by strangers.

"Oh, he is Marco Franti, but I call him 'Mark.' It's the same name, you know, and it makes him mad," said the girl, with the same suggestion of archness and co-quetry.

But all this was lost on Jarman.

"Oh, another Italian," he said, relieved. She turned away a little awkwardly when he added, "But you haven't told me YOUR name, you know."

"Cara."

"Cara,--that's 'dear' in Italian, isn't it?" he said, with a reminiscence of the op-era and a half smile.

"Yes," she said a little scornfully, "but it means Carlotta,--Charlotte, you know. Some girls call me Charley," she said hurriedly.

"I see--Cara--or Carlotta Franti."

To his surprise she burst into a peal of laughter.

"I reckon not YET. Franti is Mark's name, not mine. Mine is Murano,--Carlotta Murano. Good-by." She moved away, then stopped suddenly and said, "I'm comin' again some time when the thing is working," and with a nod of her head, ran away. He looked after her; could see the outlines of her youthful figure in her slim cotton gown,--limp and clinging in the damp sea air, and the sudden revelation of her bare ankles thrust stockingless into canvas shoes.

He went back into his cabin, when presently his attention was engrossed by an incoming vessel. He made the signals, half expecting, almost hoping, that the girl would return to watch him. But her figure was already lost in the sand dunes. Yet he fancied he still heard the echoes of her voice and his own in this cabin which had so long been dumb and voiceless, and he now started at every sound. For the first time he became aware of the dreadful disorder and untidiness of its uninvaded privacy. He could scarcely believe he had been living with his stove, his bed, and cooking utensils all in one corner of the barnlike room, and he began to put them "to rights" in a rough, hard formality, strongly suggestive of his convict experience. He rolled up his blankets into a hard cylinder at the head of his cot. He scraped out his kettles and saucepans, and even "washed down" the floor, afterwards sprinkling clean dry sand, hot with the noonday sunshine, on its half-dried boards. In arranging these domestic details he had to change the position of a little mirror; and glancing at it for the first time in many days, he was dissatisfied with his straggling beard,--grown during his voyage from Australia,--and although he had retained it as a disguise, he at once shaved it off, leaving only a mustache, and revealing a face from which a healthier life and out-of-door existence had removed the last traces of vice and dissipation. But he did not know it.

All the next day he thought of his fair visitor, and found himself often repeating her odd remark that she was "not that kind of girl," with a smile that was alternately significant or vacant. Evidently she could take care of herself, he thought, although her very good looks no doubt had exposed her to the rude attentions of fishermen or the common drift of San Francisco wharves. Perhaps this was why her father brought her here. When the day passed and she came not, he began vaguely to wonder if he had been rude to her. Perhaps he had taken her simple remark too seriously; perhaps she had expected he would only laugh, and had found him dull and stupid. Perhaps he had thrown away an opportunity. An opportunity for what? To renew his old life and habits? No, no! The horrors of his recent imprisonment and escape were still too fresh in his memory; he was not safe yet. Then he wondered if he had not grown spiritless and pigeon-livered in his solitude and loneliness. The next day he searched for her with his glass, and saw her playing with one of the children on the beach,--a very picture of child or nymphlike innocence. Perhaps it was because she was not "that kind of girl" that she had attracted him. He laughed bitterly. Yes; that was very funny; he, an escaped convict, drawn towards honest, simple innocence! Yet he knew--he was positive--he had not thought of any ill when he spoke to her. He took a singular, a ridiculous pride in and credit to himself for that. He repeated it incessantly to himself. Then what made her angry? Himself! The devil! Did he carry, then, the record of his past life forever in his face--in his speech--in his manners? The thought made him sullen. The next day he would not look towards the shore; it was wonderful what excitement and satisfaction he got out of that strange act of self-denial; it made the day seem full that had been so vacant before; yet he could not tell why or wherefore. He felt injured, but he rather liked it. Yet in the night he was struck with the idea that she might have gone back to San Francisco, and he lay awake longing for the morning light to satisfy him. Yet when the fog cleared, and from a nearer point, behind a sand dune, he discovered, by the aid of his glass, that she was seated on the sun-warmed sands combing out her long hair like a mermaid, he immediately returned to the cabin, and that morning looked no more that way. In the afternoon, there being no sails in sight, he turned aside from the bay and walked westward towards the ocean, halting only at the league-long line of foam which marked the breaking Pacific surges. Here he was surprised to see a little child, half-naked, following barefooted the creeping line of spume, or running after the detached and quivering scraps of foam that chased each other over the wet sand, and only a little further on, to come upon Cara herself, sitting with her elbows on her knees and her round chin in her hands, apparently gazing over the waste of waters before her. A sudden and inexplicable shyness overtook him. He hesitated, and stepped half-hidden in a gully between the sand dunes.

As yet he had not been observed; the young girl called to the child and, suddenly rising, threw off her red cap and shawl and quietly began to disrobe herself. A couple of coarse towels were at her feet. Jarman instantly comprehended that she was going to bathe with the child. She undoubtedly knew as well as he did that she was safe in that solitude; that no one could intrude upon her privacy from the bay shore, nor from the desolate inland trail to the sea, without her knowledge. Of his own contiguity she had evidently taken no thought, believing him safely housed in his cabin beside the semaphore. She lifted her hands, and with a sudden movement shook out her long hair and let it fall down her back at the same moment that her unloosened blouse began to slip from her shoulders. Richard Jarman turned quickly and walked noiselessly and rapidly away, until the little hillock had shut out the beach.

His retreat was as sudden, unreasoning, and unpremeditated as his intrusion. It was not like himself, he knew, and yet it was as perfectly instinctive and natural as if he had intruded upon a sister. In the South Seas he had seen native girls diving beside the vessels for coins, but they had provoked no such instinct as that which possessed him now. More than that, he swept a quick, wrathful glance along the horizon on either side, and then, mounting a remote hillock which still hid him from the beach, he sat there and kept watch and ward. From time to time the strong sea-breeze brought him the sound of infantine screams and shouts of girlish laughter from the unseen shore; he only looked the more keenly and suspiciously for any wandering trespasser, and did not turn his head. He lay there nearly half an hour, and when the sounds had ceased, rose and made his way slowly back to the cabin. He had not gone many yards before he heard the twitter of voices and smothered laughter behind him. He turned; it was Cara and the child,--a girl of six or seven. Cara's face was rosy,--possibly from her bath, and possibly from some shame-faced consciousness. He slackened his pace, and as they ranged beside him said, "Good-morning!"

"Lord!" said Cara, stifling another laugh, "we didn't know you were around; we thought you were always 'tending your telegraph, didn't we, Lucy?" (to the child, who was convulsed with mirth and sheepishness). "Why, we've been taking a wash in the sea." She tried to gather up her long hair, which had been left to stray over her shoulders and dry in the sunlight, and even made a slight pretense of trying to conceal the wet towels they were carrying.

Jarman did not laugh. "If you had told me," he said gravely, "I could have kept watch for you with my glass while you were there. I could see further than you."

"Tould you see US?" asked the little girl, with hopeful vivacity.

"No!" said Jarman, with masterly evasion. "There are little sandhills between this and the beach."

"Then how tould other people see us?" persisted the child.

Jarman could see that the older girl was evidently embarrassed, and changed the subject. "I sometimes go out," he said, "when I can see there are no vessels in sight, and I take ray glass with me. I can always get back in time to make signals. I thought, in fact," he said, glancing at Cara's brightening face, "that I might get as far as your house on the shore some day." To his surprise, her embarrassment suddenly seemed to increase, although she had looked relieved before, and she did not reply. After a moment she said abruptly:--

"Did you ever see the sea-lions?"

"No," said Jarman.

"Not the big ones on Seal Rock, beyond the cliffs?" continued the girl, in real astonishment.

"No," repeated Jarman. "I never walked in that direction." He vaguely remembered that they were a curiosity which sometimes attracted parties thither, and for that reason he had avoided the spot.

"Why, I have sailed all around the rock in father's boat," continued Cara, with importance. "That's the best way to see 'em, and folks from Frisco sometimes takes a sail out there just on purpose,--it's too sandy to walk or drive there. But it's only a step from here. Look here!" she said suddenly, and frankly opening her fine eyes upon him. "I'm going to take Lucy there to-morrow, and I'll show you." Jarman felt his cheeks flush quickly with a pleasure that embarrassed him. "It won't take long," added Cara, mistaking his momentary hesitation, "and you can leave your telegraph alone. Nobody will be there, so no one will see you and nobody know it."

He would have gone then, anyway, he knew, yet in his absurd self-consciousness he was glad that her last suggestion had relieved him of a sense of reckless compliance. He assented eagerly, when with a wave of her hand, a flash of her white teeth, and the same abruptness she had shown at their last parting, she caught Lucy by the arm and darted away in a romping race to her dwelling. Jarman started after her. He had not wanted to go to her father's house particularly, but why was SHE evidently as averse to it? With the subtle pleasure that this admission gave him there was a faint stirring of suspicion.

It was gone when he found her and Lucy the next morning, radiant with the sunshine, before his door. The restraint of their previous meetings had been removed in some mysterious way, and they chatted gayly as they walked towards the cliffs. She asked him frankly many questions about himself, why he had come there, and if he "wasn't lonely;" she answered frankly--I fear much more frankly than he answered her--the many questions he asked her about herself and her friends. When they reached the cliffs they descended to the beach, which they found deserted. Before them--it seemed scarce a pistol shot from the shore arose a high, broad rock, beaten at its base by the long Pacific surf, on which a number of shapeless animals were uncouthly disporting. This was Seal Rock, the goal of their journey.

Yet after a few moments they no longer looked at it, but seated on the sand, with Lucy gathering shells at the water's edge, they continued their talk. Presently the talk became eager confidences, and then,--there were long and dangerous lapses of silence, when both were fain to make perfunctory talk with Lucy on the beach. After one of those silences Jarman said:--

"Do you know I rather thought yesterday you didn't want me to come to your father's house. Why was that?"

"Because Marco was there," said the girl frankly.

"What had HE to do with it?" said Jarman abruptly.

"He wants to marry me."

"And do you want to marry HIM?" said Jarman quickly.

"No," said the girl passionately.

"Why don't you get rid of him, then?"

"I can't, he's hiding here,--he's father's friend."

"Hiding? What's he been doing?"

"Stealing. Stealing gold-dust from miners. I never cared for him anyway. And I hate a thief!"

She looked up quickly. Jarman had risen to his feet, his face turned to sea.

"What are you looking at?" she said wonderingly.

"A ship," said Jarman, in a strange, hoarse voice. "I must hurry back and signal. I'm afraid I haven't even time to walk with you,--I must run for it. Good-by!"

He turned without offering his hand and ran hurriedly in the direction of the semaphore.

Cara, discomfited, turned her black eyes to the sea. But it seemed empty as before, no sail, no ship on the horizon line, only a little schooner slowly beating out of the Gate. Ah, well! It no doubt was there,--that sail,--though she could not see it; how keen and far-seeing his handsome, honest eyes were! She heaved a little sigh, and, calling Lucy to her side, began to make her way homeward. But she kept her eyes on the semaphore; it seemed to her the next thing to seeing him,--this man she was beginning to love. She waited for the gaunt arms to move with the signal of the vessel he had seen. But, strange to say, it was motionless. He must have been mistaken.

All this, however, was driven from her mind in the excitement that she found on her return thrilling her own family. They had been warned that a police boat with detectives on board had been dispatched from San Francisco to the cove. Luckily, they had managed to convey the fugitive Franti on board a coastwise schooner,-

-Cara started as she remembered the one she had seen beating out of the Gate,--and he was now safe from pursuit. Cara felt relieved; at the same time she felt a strange joy at her heart, which sent the conscious blood to her cheek. She was not thinking of the escaped Marco, but of Jarman. Later, when the police boat arrived,--whether the detectives had been forewarned of Marco's escape or not,--they contented themselves with a formal search of the little fishing-hut and departed. But their boat remained lying off the shore.

That night Cara tossed sleeplessly on her bed; she was sorry she had ever spoken of Marco to Jarman. It was unnecessary now; perhaps he disbelieved her and thought she loved Marco; perhaps that was the reason of his strange and abrupt leave-taking that afternoon. She longed for the next day, she could tell him everything now.

Towards morning she slept fitfully, but was awakened by the sound of voices on the sands outside the hut. Its flimsy structure, already warped by the fierce day-long sun, allowed her through chinks and crevices not only to recognize the voices of the detectives, but to hear distinctly what they said. Suddenly the name of Jarman struck upon her ear. She sat upright in bed, breathless.

"Are you sure it's the same man?" asked a second voice.

"Perfectly," answered the first. "He was tracked to 'Frisco, but disappeared the day he landed. We knew from our agents that he never left the bay. And when we found that somebody answering his description got the post of telegraph operator out here, we knew that we had spotted our man and the L250 sterling offered for his capture."

"But that was five months ago. Why didn't you take him then?"

"Couldn't! For we couldn't hold him without the extradition papers from Australia. We sent for 'em; they're due to-day or to-morrow on the mail steamer."

"But he might have got away at any time?"

"He couldn't without our knowing it. Don't you see? Every time the signals went up, we in San Francisco knew he was at his post. We had him safe, out here on these sandhills, as if he'd been under lock and key in 'Frisco. He was his own keeper, and reported to us."

"But since you're here and expect the papers to-morrow, why don't you 'cop' him now?"

"Because there isn't a judge in San Francisco that would hold him a moment unless he had those extradition papers before him. He'd be discharged, and escape."

"Then what are you going to do?"

"As soon as the steamer is signaled in 'Frisco, we'll board her in the bay, get the papers, and drop down upon him."

"I see; and as HE'S the signal man, the darned fool"--

"Will give the signal himself."

The laugh that followed was so cruel that the young girl shuddered. But the next moment she slipped from the bed, erect, pale, and determined.

The voices seemed gradually to retreat. She dressed herself hurriedly, and passed noiselessly through the room of her still sleeping parent, and passed out. A gray fog was lifting slowly over the sands and sea, and the police boat was gone. She no longer hesitated, but ran quickly in the direction of Jarman's cabin. As she ran, her mind seemed to be swept clear of all illusion and fancy; she saw plainly everything that had happened; she knew the mystery of Jarman's presence here,-- the secret of his life,--the dreadful cruelty of her remark to him,--the man that she knew now she loved. The sun was painting the black arms of the semaphore as she toiled over the last stretch of sand and knocked loudly at the door. There was no reply. She knocked again; the cabin was silent. Had he already fled?--and without seeing her and knowing all! She tried the handle of the door; it yielded; she stepped boldly into the room, with his name upon her lips. He was lying fully dressed upon his couch. She ran eagerly to his side and stopped. It needed only a single glance at his congested face, his lips parted with his heavy breath, to see that the man was hopelessly, helplessly drunk!

Yet even then, without knowing that it was her thoughtless speech which had driven him to seek this foolish oblivion of remorse and sorrow, she saw only his HELPLESSNESS. She tried in vain to rouse him; he only muttered a few incoherent words and sank back again. She looked despairingly around. Something must be done; the steamer might be visible at any moment. Ah, yes,--the telescope! She seized it and swept the horizon. There was a faint streak of haze against the line of sea and sky, abreast the Golden Gate. He had once told her what it meant. It WAS the steamer! A sudden thought leaped into her clear and active brain. If the police boat should chance to see that haze too, and saw no warning signal from the semaphore, they would suspect something. That signal must be made, BUT NOT THE RIGHT ONE! She remembered quickly how he had explained to her the difference between the signals for a coasting steamer and the one that brought the mails. At that distance the police boat could not detect whether the semaphore's arms were extended to perfect right angles for the mail steamer, or if the left arm slightly deflected for a coasting steamer. She ran out to the windlass and seized the crank. For a moment it defied her strength; she redoubled her efforts: it began to creak and groan, the great arms were slowly uplifted, and the signal made.

But the familiar sounds of the moving machinery had pierced through Jarman's sluggish consciousness as no other sound in heaven or earth could have done, and awakened him to the one dominant sense he had left,--the habit of duty. She heard him roll from the bed with an oath, stumble to the door, and saw him dash forward with an affrighted face, and plunge his head into a bucket of water. He emerged from it pale and dripping, but with the full light of reason and consciousness in his eyes. He started when he saw her; even then she would have fled, but he caught her firmly by the wrist.

Then with a hurried, trembling voice she told him all and everything. He listened in silence, and only at the end raised her hand gravely to his lips.

"And now," she added tremulously, "you must fly--quick--at once; or it will be too late!"

But Richard Jarman walked slowly to the door of his cabin, still holding her hand, and said quietly, pointing to his only chair:--

"Sit down; we must talk first."

What they said was never known, but a few moments later they left the cabin, Jarman carrying in a small bag all his possessions, and Cara leaning on his arm. An hour later the priest of the Mission Dolores was called upon to unite in matrimony a frank, honest-looking sailor and an Italian gypsy-looking girl. There were many hasty unions in those days, and the Holy Church was only too glad to be able to give them its legal indorsement. But the good Padre was a little sorry for the honest sailor, and gave the girl some serious advice.

The San Francisco papers the next morning threw some dubious light upon the matter in a paragraph headed, "Another Police Fiasco."

"We understand that the indefatigable police of San Francisco, after ascertaining that Marco Franti, the noted gold-dust thief, was hiding on the shore near the Presidio, proceeded there with great solemnity, and arrived, as usual, a few hours after their man had escaped. But the climax of incapacity was reached when, as it is alleged, the sweetheart of the absconding Franti, and daughter of a brother fisher-man, eloped still later, and joined her lover under the very noses of the police. The attempt of the detectives to excuse themselves at headquarters by reporting that they were also on the track of an alleged escaped Sydney Duck was received with the derision and skepticism it deserved, as it seemed that these worthies mistook the mail steamer, which they should have boarded to get certain extradition papers, for a coasting steamer."

*****

It was not until four years later that Murano was delighted to recognize in the husband of his long-lost daughter a very rich cattle-owner in Southern California, called Jarman; but he never knew that he had been an escaped convict from Syd-ney, who had lately received a full pardon through the instrumentality of divers distinguished people in Australia.

AN ESMERALDA OF ROCKY CANYON

It is to be feared that the hero of this chronicle began life as an impostor. He was offered to the credulous and sympathetic family of a San Francisco citizen as a lamb, who, unless bought as a playmate for the children, would inevitably pass into the butcher's hands. A combination of refined sensibility and urban ignorance of nature prevented them from discerning certain glaring facts that betrayed his caprid origin. So a ribbon was duly tied round his neck, and in pleasing emulation of the legendary "Mary," he was taken to school by the confiding children. Here, alas the fraud was discovered, and history was reversed by his being turned out by the teacher, because he was NOT "a lamb at school." Nevertheless, the kind-hearted mother of the family persisted in retaining him, on the plea that he might yet become "useful." To her husband's feeble suggestion of "gloves," she returned a scornful negative, and spoke of the weakly infant of a neighbor, who might later receive nourishment from this providential animal. But even this hope was destroyed by the eventual discovery of his sex. Nothing remained now but to accept him as an ordinary kid, and to find amusement in his accomplishments,-- eating, climbing, and butting. It must be confessed that these were of a superior quality; a capacity to eat everything from a cambric handkerchief to an election poster, an agility which brought him even to the roofs of houses, and a power of overturning by a single push the chubbiest child who opposed him, made him a fearful joy to the nursery. This last quality was incautiously developed in him by a negro boy-servant, who, later, was hurriedly propelled down a flight of stairs by his too proficient scholar. Having once tasted victory, "Billy" needed no further incitement to his performances. The small wagon which he sometimes consented to draw for the benefit of the children never hindered his attempts to butt the passer-by. On the contrary, on well-known scientific principles he added the impact of the bodies of the children projected over his head in his charge, and the infelicitous pedestrian found himself not only knocked off his legs by Billy, but bombarded by the whole nursery.

Delightful as was this recreation to juvenile limbs, it was felt to be dangerous to the adult public. Indignant protestations were made, and as Billy could not be kept in the house, he may be said to have at last butted himself out of that sympathetic family and into a hard and unfeeling world. One morning he broke his tether in the small back yard. For several days thereafter he displayed himself in guilty freedom on the tops of adjacent walls and outhouses. The San Francisco suburb where his credulous protectors lived was still in a volcanic state of disruption, caused by the grading of new streets through rocks and sandhills. In consequence the roofs of some houses were on the level of the doorsteps of others, and were especially adapted to Billy's performances. One afternoon, to the admiring and perplexed eyes of the nursery, he was discovered standing on the apex of a neighbor's new Elizabethan chimney, on a space scarcely larger than the crown of a hat, calmly surveying the world beneath him. High infantile voices appealed to him in vain; baby arms were outstretched to him in hopeless invitation; he remained exalted and obdurate, like Milton's hero, probably by his own merit "raised to that bad eminence." Indeed, there was already something Satanic in his budding horns and pointed mask as the smoke curled softly around him. Then he appropriately vanished, and San Francisco knew him no more. At the same time, however, one Owen M'Ginnis, a neighboring sandhill squatter, also disappeared, leaving San Francisco for the southern mines, and he was said to have taken Billy with him,--for no conceivable reason except for companionship. Howbeit, it was the turning-point of Billy's career; such restraint as kindness, civilization, or even policemen had exercised upon his nature was gone. He retained, I fear, a certain wicked intelligence, picked up in San Francisco with the newspapers and theatrical and election posters he had consumed. He reappeared at Rocky Canyon among the miners as an exceedingly agile chamois, with the low cunning of a satyr. That was all that civilization had done for him!

If Mr. M'Ginnis had fondly conceived that he would make Billy "useful," as well as companionable, he was singularly mistaken. Horses and mules were scarce in Rocky Canyon, and he attempted to utilize Billy by making him draw a small cart, laden with auriferous earth, from his claim to the river. Billy, rapidly gaining strength, was quite equal to the task, but alas! not his inborn propensity. An incautious gesture from the first passing miner Billy chose to construe into the usual challenge. Lowering his head, from which his budding horns had been already pruned by his master, he instantly went for his challenger, cart and all. Again the scientific law already pointed out prevailed. With the shock of the onset the entire contents of the cart arose and poured over the astonished miner, burying him from sight. In any other but a Californian mining-camp such a propensity in a draught animal would have been condemned, on account of the damage and suffering it entailed, but in Rocky Canyon it proved unprofitable to the owner from the very amusement and interest it excited. Miners lay in wait for Billy with a "greenhorn," or new-comer, whom they would put up to challenge the animal by some indiscreet gesture. In this way hardly a cartload of "pay-gravel" ever arrived safely at its destination, and the unfortunate M'Ginnis was compelled to withdraw Billy as a beast of burden. It was whispered that so great had his propensity become, under repeated provocation, that M'Ginnis himself was no longer safe. Going ahead of his cart one day to remove a fallen bough from the trail, Billy construed the act of stooping into a playful challenge from his master,--with the inevitable result.

The next day M'Ginnis appeared with a wheelbarrow, but without Billy. From that day he was relegated to the rocky crags above the camp, from whence he was only lured occasionally by the mischievous miners, who wished to exhibit his peculiar performances. For although Billy had ample food and sustenance among the crags, he had still a civilized longing for posters; and whenever a circus, a concert, or a political meeting was "billed" in the settlement, he was on hand while the paste was yet fresh and succulent. In this way it was averred that he once removed a gigantic theatre bill setting forth the charms of the "Sacramento Pet," and being caught in the act by the advance agent, was pursued through the main street, carrying the damp bill on his horns, eventually affixing it, after his own peculiar fashion, on the back of Judge Boompointer, who was standing in front of his own court-house.

In connection with the visits of this young lady another story concerning Billy survives in the legends of Rocky Canyon. Colonel Starbottle was at that time passing through the settlement on election business, and it was part of his chivalrous admiration for the sex to pay a visit to the pretty actress. The single waiting-room of the little hotel gave upon the veranda, which was also level with the street. After a brief yet gallant interview, in which he oratorically expressed the gratitude of the settlement with old-fashioned Southern courtesy, Colonel Starbottle lifted the chubby little hand of the "Pet" to his lips, and, with a low bow, backed out upon the veranda. But the Pet was astounded by his instant reappearance, and by his apparently casting himself passionately and hurriedly at her feet! It is needless to say that he was followed closely by Billy, who from the street had casually noticed him, and construed his novel exit into an ungentlemanly challenge.

Billy's visits, however, became less frequent, and as Rocky Canyon underwent the changes incidental to mining settlements, he was presently forgotten in the invasion of a few Southwestern families, and the adoption of amusements less practical and turbulent than he had afforded. It was alleged that he was still seen in the more secluded fastnesses of the mountains, having reverted to a wild state, and it was suggested by one or two of the more adventurous that he might yet become edible, and a fair object of chase. A traveler through the Upper Pass of the canyon related how he had seen a savage-looking, hairy animal like a small elk perched upon inaccessible rocks, but always out of gunshot. But these and other legends were set at naught and overthrown by an unexpected incident.

The Pioneer Coach was toiling up the long grade towards Skinners Pass when Yuba Bill suddenly pulled up, with his feet on the brake.

"Jimminy!" he ejaculated, drawing a deep breath.

The startled passenger beside him on the box followed the direction of his eyes. Through an opening in the wayside pines he could see, a few hundred yards away, a cuplike hollow in the hillside of the vividest green. In the centre a young girl of fifteen or sixteen was dancing and keeping step to the castanet "click" of a pair of "bones," such as negro minstrels use, held in her hands above her head. But, more singular still, a few paces before her a large goat, with its neck roughly wreathed with flowers and vines, was taking ungainly bounds and leaps in imitation of its companion. The wild background of the Sierras, the pastoral hollow, the incongruousness of the figures, and the vivid color of the girl's red flannel petticoat showing beneath her calico skirt, that had been pinned around her waist, made a striking picture, which by this time had attracted all eyes. Perhaps the dancing of the girl suggested a negro "break-down" rather than any known sylvan measure; but all this, and even the clatter of the bones, was made gracious by the distance.

"Esmeralda! by the living Harry!" shouted the excited passenger on the box.

Yuba Bill took his feet off the brake, and turned a look of deep scorn upon his companion as he gathered the reins again.

"It's that blanked goat, outer Rocky Canyon beyond, and Polly Harkness! How did she ever come to take up with HIM?"

Nevertheless, as soon as the coach reached Rocky Canyon, the story was quickly told by the passengers, corroborated by Yuba Bill, and highly colored by the observer on the box-seat. Harkness was known to be a new-comer who lived with his wife and only daughter on the other side of Skinners Pass. He was a "logger" and charcoal-burner, who had eaten his way into the serried ranks of pines below the pass, and established in these efforts an almost insurmountable cordon of fallen trees, stripped bark, and charcoal pits around the clearing where his rude log hut stood,--which kept his seclusion unbroken. He was said to be a half-savage mountaineer from Georgia, in whose rude fastnesses he had distilled unlawful whiskey, and that his tastes and habits unfitted him for civilization. His wife chewed and smoked; he was believed to make a fiery brew of his own from acorns and pine nuts; he seldom came to Rocky Canyon except for provisions; his logs were slipped down a "shoot" or slide to the river, where they voyaged once a month to a distant mill, but HE did not accompany them. The daughter, seldom seen at Rocky Canyon, was a half-grown girl, brown as autumn fern, wild-eyed, disheveled, in a homespun skirt, sunbonnet, and boy's brogans. Such were the plain facts which skeptical Rocky Canyon opposed to the passengers' legends. Nevertheless, some of the younger miners found it not out of their way to go over Skinners Pass on the journey to the river, but with what success was not told. It was said, however, that a celebrated New York artist, making a tour of California, was on the coach one day going through the pass, and preserved the memory of what he saw there in a well-known picture entitled "Dancing Nymph and Satyr," said by competent critics to be "replete with the study of Greek life." This did not affect Rocky Canyon, where the study of mythology was presumably displaced by an experience of more wonderful flesh-and-blood people, but later it was remembered with some significance.

Among the improvements already noted, a zinc and wooden chapel had been erected in the main street, where a certain popular revivalist preacher of a peculiar

Southwestern sect regularly held exhortatory services. His rude emotional power over his ignorant fellow-sectarians was well known, while curiosity drew others. His effect upon the females of his flock was hysterical and sensational. Women prematurely aged by frontier drudgery and child-bearing, girls who had known only the rigors and pains of a half-equipped, ill-nourished youth in their battling with the hard realities of nature around them, all found a strange fascination in the extravagant glories and privileges of the unseen world he pictured to them, which they might have found in the fairy tales and nursery legends of civilized children, had they known them. Personally he was not attractive; his thin pointed face, and bushy hair rising on either side of his square forehead in two rounded knots, and his long, straggling, wiry beard dropping from a strong neck and shoulders, were indeed of a common Southwestern type; yet in him they suggested something more. This was voiced by a miner who attended his first service, and as the Reverend Mr. Withholder rose in the pulpit, the former was heard to audibly ejaculate, "Dod blasted!--if it ain't Billy!" But when on the following Sunday, to everybody's astonishment, Polly Harkness, in a new white muslin frock and broad-brimmed Leghorn hat, appeared before the church door with the real Billy, and exchanged conversation with the preacher, the likeness was appalling.

I grieve to say that the goat was at once christened by Rocky Canyon as "The Reverend Billy," and the minister himself was Billy's "brother." More than that, when an attempt was made by outsiders, during the service, to inveigle the tethered goat into his old butting performances, and he took not the least notice of their insults and challenges, the epithet "blanked hypocrite" was added to his title.

Had he really reformed? Had his pastoral life with his nymph-like mistress completely cured him of his pugnacious propensity, or had he simply found it was inconsistent with his dancing, and seriously interfered with his "fancy steps"? Had he found tracts and hymn-books were as edible as theatre posters? These were questions that Rocky canyon discussed lightly, although there was always the more serious mystery of the relations of the Reverend Mr. Withholder, Polly Harkness, and the goat towards each other. The appearance of Polly at church was no doubt due to the minister's active canvass of the districts. But had he ever heard of Polly's dancing with the goat? And where in this plain, angular, badly dressed Polly was hidden that beautiful vision of the dancing nymph which had enthralled so many? And when had Billy ever given any suggestion of his Terpsichorean abilities--before or since? Were there any "points" of the kind to be discerned in him now? None! Was it not more probable that the Reverend Mr. Withholder had himself been dancing with Polly, and been mistaken for the goat? Passengers who could have been so deceived with regard to Polly's beauty might have as easily mistaken the minister for Billy. About this time another incident occurred which increased the mystery.

The only male in the settlement who apparently dissented from the popular opinion regarding Polly was a new-comer, Jack Filgee. While discrediting her performance with the goat,--which he had never seen,--he was evidently greatly prepossessed with the girl herself. Unfortunately, he was equally addicted to drinking, and as he was exceedingly shy and timid when sober, and quite unpresentable at other times, his wooing, if it could be so called, progressed but slowly. Yet when he found that Polly went to church, he listened so far to the exhortations of the Reverend Mr. Withholder as to promise to come to "Bible class" immediately after the Sunday service. It was a hot afternoon, and Jack, who had kept sober for two days, incautiously fortified himself for the ordeal by taking a drink before arriving. He was nervously early, and immediately took a seat in the empty church near the open door. The quiet of the building, the drowsy buzzing of flies, and perhaps the soporific effect of the liquor caused his eyes to close and his head to fall forward on his breast repeatedly. He was recovering himself for the fourth time when he suddenly received a violent cuff on the ear, and was knocked backward off the bench on which he was sitting. That was all he knew.

He picked himself up with a certain dignity, partly new to him, and partly the result of his condition, and staggered, somewhat bruised and disheveled, to the nearest saloon. Here a few frequenters who had seen him pass, who knew his errand and the devotion to Polly which had induced it, exhibited a natural concern.

"How's things down at the gospel shop?" said one. "Look as ef you'd been wrastlin' with the Sperit, Jack!"

"Old man must hev exhorted pow'ful," said another, glancing at his disordered Sunday attire.

"Ain't be'n hevin' a row with Polly? I'm told she slings an awful left."

Jack, instead of replying, poured out a dram of whiskey, drank it, and putting down his glass, leaned heavily against the counter as he surveyed his questioners with a sorrow chastened by reproachful dignity.

"I'm a stranger here, gentlemen," he said slowly "ye've known me only a little; but ez ye've seen me both blind drunk and sober, I reckon ye've caught on to my gin'ral gait! Now I wanter put it to you, ez fair-minded men, ef you ever saw me strike a parson?"

"No," said a chorus of sympathetic voices. The barkeeper, however, with a swift recollection of Polly and the Reverend Withholder, and some possible contingent jealousy in Jack, added prudently, "Not yet."

The chorus instantly added reflectively, "Well, no not yet."

"Did ye ever," continued Jack solemnly, "know me to cuss, sass, bully-rag, or say anything agin parsons, or the church?"

"No," said the crowd, overthrowing prudence in curiosity, "ye never did,--we swear it! And now, what's up?"

"I ain't what you call 'a member in good standin','" he went on, artistically pro-tracting his climax. "I ain't be'n convicted o' sin; I ain't 'a meek an' lowly follower;' I ain't be'n exactly what I orter be'n; I hevn't lived anywhere up to my lights; but is thet a reason why a parson should strike me?"

"Why? What? When did he? Who did?" asked the eager crowd, with one voice.

Jack then painfully related how he had been invited by the Reverend Mr. With-holder to attend the Bible class. How he had arrived early, and found the church empty. How he had taken a seat near the door to be handy when the parson came. How he just felt "kinder kam and good," listenin' to the flies buzzing, and must have fallen asleep,--only he pulled himself up every time,--though, after all, it warn't no crime to fall asleep in an empty church! IIow "all of a suddent" the parson came in, "give him a clip side o' the head," and knocked him off the bench, and left him there!

"But what did he SAY?" queried the crowd.

"Nuthin'. Afore I could get up, he got away."

"Are you sure it was him?" they asked. "You know you SAY you was asleep."

"Am I sure?" repeated Jack scornfully. "Don't I know thet face and beard? Didn't I feel it hangin' over me?"

"What are you going to do about it?" continued the crowd eagerly.

"Wait till he comes out--and you'll see," said Jack, with dignity.

This was enough for the crowd; they gathered excitedly at the door, where Jack was already standing, looking towards the church. The moments dragged slowly; it might be a long meeting. Suddenly the church door opened and a figure appeared, looking up and down the street. Jack colored--he recognized Polly--and stepped out into the road. The crowd delicately, but somewhat disappointedly, drew back in the saloon. They did not care to interfere in THAT sort of thing.

Polly saw him, and came hurriedly towards him. She was holding something in her hand.

"I picked this up on the church floor," she said shyly, "so I reckoned you HAD be'n there,--though the parson said you hadn't,--and I just excused myself and ran out to give it ye. It's yourn, ain't it?" She held up a gold specimen pin, which he had put on in honor of the occasion. "I had a harder time, though, to git this yer,--it's yourn too,--for Billy was laying down in the yard, back o' the church, and just comf'bly swallerin' it."

"Who?" said Jack quickly.

"Billy,--my goat."

Jack drew a long breath, and glanced back at the saloon. "Ye ain't goin' back to class now, are ye?" he said hurriedly. "Ef you ain't, I'll--I'll see ye home."

"I don't mind," said Polly demurely, "if it ain't takin' ye outer y'ur way."

Jack offered his arm, and hurrying past the saloon, the happy pair were soon on the road to Skinners Pass.

Jack did not, I regret to say, confess his blunder, but left the Reverend Mr. Withholder to remain under suspicion of having committed an unprovoked assault and battery. It was characteristic of Rocky Canyon, however, that this suspicion, far from injuring his clerical reputation, incited a respect that had been hitherto denied him. A man who could hit out straight from the shoulder had, in the language of the critics, "suthin' in him." Oddly enough, the crowd that had at first sympathized with Jack now began to admit provocations. His subsequent silence, a disposition when questioned on the subject to smile inanely, and, later, when insidiously asked if he had ever seen Polly dancing with the goat, his bursting into uproarious laughter completely turned the current of opinion against him. The public mind, however, soon became engrossed by a more interesting incident.

The Reverend Mr. Withholder had organized a series of Biblical tableaux at Skinnerstown for the benefit of his church. Illustrations were to be given of "Rebecca at the Well," "The Finding of Moses," "Joseph and his Brethren;" but Rocky Canyon was more particularly excited by the announcement that Polly Harkness would personate "Jephthah's Daughter." On the evening of the performance, however, it was found that this tableau had been withdrawn and another substituted, for reasons not given. Rocky Canyon, naturally indignant at this omission to represent native talent, indulged in a hundred wild surmises. But it was generally believed that Jack Filgee's revengeful animosity to the Reverend Mr. Withholder was at the bottom of it. Jack, as usual, smiled inanely, but nothing was to be got from him. It was not until a few days later, when another incident crowned the climax of these mysteries, that a full disclosure came from his lips.

One morning a flaming poster was displayed at Rocky Canyon, with a charming picture of the "Sacramento Pet" in the briefest of skirts, disporting with a tambourine before a goat garlanded with flowers, who bore, however, an undoubted likeness to Billy. The text in enormous letters, and bristling with points of admiration, stated that the "Pet" would appear as "Esmeralda," assisted by a performing goat, especially trained by the gifted actress. The goat would dance, play cards, and perform those tricks of magic familiar to the readers of Victor Hugo's beautiful story of the "Hunchback of Notre Dame," and finally knock down and overthrow the designing seducer, Captain Phoebus. The marvelous spectacle would be produced under the patronage of the Hon. Colonel Starbottle and the Mayor of Skinnerstown.

As all Rocky Canyon gathered open-mouthed around the poster, Jack demurely joined the group. Every eye was turned upon him.

"It don't look as if yer Polly was in THIS show, any more than she was in the tablows," said one, trying to conceal his curiosity under a slight sneer. "She don't seem to be doin' any dancin'!"

"She never DID any dancin'," said Jack, with a smile.

"Never DID! Then what was all these yarns about her dancin' up at the pass?"

"It was the Sacramento Pet who did all the dancin'; Polly only LENT the goat. Ye see, the Pet kinder took a shine to Billy arter he bowled Starbottle over thet day at the hotel, and she thought she might teach him tricks. So she DID, doing all her teachin' and stage-rehearsin' up there at the pass, so's to be outer sight, and keep this thing dark. She bribed Polly to lend her the goat and keep her secret, and Polly never let on a word to anybody but me."

"Then it was the Pet that Yuba Bill saw dancin' from the coach?"

"Yes."

"And that yer artist from New York painted as an 'Imp and Satire'?"

"Yes."

"Then that's how Polly didn't show up in them tablows at Skinnerstown? It was Withholder who kinder smelt a rat, eh? and found out it was only a theayter gal all along that did the dancin'?"

"Well, you see," said Jack, with affected hesitation, "thet's another yarn. I don't know mebbe ez I oughter tell it. Et ain't got anything to do with this advertisement o' the Pet, and might be rough on old man Withholder! Ye mustn't ask me, boys."

But there was that in his eye, and above all in this lazy procrastination of the true humorist when he is approaching his climax, which rendered the crowd clamorous and unappeasable. They WOULD have the story!

Seeing which, Jack leaned back against a rock with great gravity, put his hands in his pockets, looked discontentedly at the ground, and began: "You see, boys, old Parson Withholder had heard all these yarns about Polly and thet trick-goat, and he kinder reckoned that she might do for some one of his tablows. So he axed her if she'd mind standin' with the goat and a tambourine for Jephthah's Daughter, at about the time when old Jeph comes home, sailin' in and vowin' he'll kill the first thing he sees,--jest as it is in the Bible story. Well, Polly didn't like to say it wasn't HER that performed with the goat, but the Pet, for thet would give the Pet dead away; so Polly agrees to come thar with the goat and rehearse the tablow. Well, Polly's thar, a little shy; and Billy,--you bet HE'S all there, and ready for the fun; but the darned fool who plays Jephthah ain't worth shucks, and when HE comes in he does nothin' but grin at Polly and seem skeert at the goat. This makes old Withholder jest wild, and at last he goes on the platform hisself to show them how the thing oughter be done. So he comes bustlin' and prancin' in, and ketches sight o' Polly dancin' in with the goat to welcome him; and then he clasps his hands--so-- and drops on his knees, and hangs down his head--so--and sez, 'Me chyld! me vow! Oh, heavens!' But jest then Billy--who's gettin' rather tired o' all this foolishness--kinder slues round on his hind legs, and ketches sight o' the parson!" Jack paused a moment, and thrusting his hands still deeper in his pockets, said lazily, "I don't know if you fellers have noticed how much old Withholder looks like Billy?"

There was a rapid and impatient chorus of "Yes! yes!" and "Go on!"

"Well," continued Jack, "when Billy sees Withholder kneelin' thar with his head down, he gives a kind o' joyous leap and claps his hoofs together, ez much ez to say, 'I'm on in this scene,' drops his own head, and jest lights out for the parson!"

"And butts him clean through the side scenes into the street," interrupted a delighted auditor.

But Jack's face never changed. "Ye think so?" he said gravely. "But thet's jest whar ye slip up; and thet's jest whar Billy slipped up!" he added slowly. "Mebbe ye've noticed, too, thet the parson's built kinder solid about the head and shoulders. It mought hev be'n thet, or thet Billy didn't get a fair start, but thet goat went down on his fore legs like a shot, and the parson gave one heave, and jest scooted him off the platform! Then the parson reckoned thet this yer 'tablow' had better be left out, as thar didn't seem to be any other man who could play Jephthah, and it wasn't dignified for HIM to take the part. But the parson allowed thet it might be a great moral lesson to Billy!"

And it WAS, for from that moment Billy never attempted to butt again. He performed with great docility later on in the Pet's engagement at Skinnerstown; he played a distinguished role throughout the provinces; he had had the advantages of Art from "the Pet," and of Simplicity from Polly, but only Rocky Canyon knew that his real education had come with his first rehearsal with the Reverend Mr. Withholder.

DICK SPINDLER'S FAMILY CHRISTMAS

There was surprise and sometimes disappointment in Rough and Ready, when it was known that Dick Spindler intended to give a "family" Christmas party at his own house. That he should take an early opportunity to celebrate his good fortune and show hospitality was only expected from the man who had just made a handsome "strike" on his claim; but that it should assume so conservative, old-fashioned, and respectable a form was quite unlooked-for by Rough and Ready, and was thought by some a trifle pretentious. There were not half-a-dozen families in Rough and Ready; nobody ever knew before that Spindler had any relations, and this "ringing in" of strangers to the settlement seemed to indicate at least a lack of public spirit. "He might," urged one of his critics, "hev given the boys,--that had worked alongside o' him in the ditches by day, and slung lies with him around the camp-fire by night,--he might hev given them a square 'blow out,' and kep' the leavin's for his old Spindler crew, just as other families do. Why, when old man Scudder had his house-raisin' last year, his family lived for a week on what was left over, arter the boys had waltzed through the house that night,--and the Scudders warn't strangers, either." It was also evident that there was an uneasy feeling that Spindler's action indicated an unhallowed leaning towards the minority of respectability and exclusiveness, and a desertion--without the excuse of matrimony--of the convivial and independent bachelor majority of Rough and Ready.

"Ef he was stuck after some gal and was kinder looking ahead, I'd hev understood it," argued another critic.

"Don't ye be too sure he ain't," said Uncle Jim Starbuck gloomily. "Ye'll find that some blamed woman is at the bottom of this yer 'family' gathering. That and trouble ez almost all they're made for!"

There happened to be some truth in this dark prophecy, but none of the kind that the misogynist supposed. In fact, Spindler had called a few evenings before at the house of the Rev. Mr. Saltover, and Mrs. Saltover, having one of her "Saleratus headaches," had turned him over to her widow sister, Mrs. Huldy Price, who obediently bestowed upon him that practical and critical attention which she divided with the stocking she was darning. She was a woman of thirty-five, of singular nerve and practical wisdom, who had once smuggled her wounded husband home from a border affray, calmly made coffee for his deceived pursuers while he lay hidden in the loft, walked four miles for that medical assistance which arrived too late to save him, buried him secretly in his own "quarter section," with only one other witness and mourner, and so saved her position and property in that wild community, who believed he had fled. There was very little of this experience to be traced in her round, fresh-colored brunette cheek, her calm black eyes, set in a prickly hedge of stiff lashes, her plump figure, or her frank, courageous laugh. The latter appeared as a smile when she welcomed Mr. Spindler. "She hadn't seen him for a coon's age," but "reckoned he was busy fixin' up his new house."

"Well, yes," said Spindler, with a slight hesitation, "ye see, I'm reckonin' to hev a kinder Christmas gatherin' of my"--he was about to say "folks," but dismissed it for "relations," and finally settled upon "relatives" as being more correct in a preacher's house.

Mrs. Price thought it a very good idea. Christmas was the natural season for the family to gather to "see who's here and who's there, who's gettin' on and who isn't, and who's dead and buried. It was lucky for them who were so placed that they could do so and be joyful." Her invincible philosophy probably carried her past any dangerous recollections of the lonely grave in Kansas, and holding up the stocking to the light, she glanced cheerfully along its level to Mr. Spindler's embarrassed face by the fire.

"Well, I can't say much ez to that," responded Spindler, still awkwardly, "for you see I don't know much about it anyway."

"How long since you've seen 'em?" asked Mrs. Price, apparently addressing herself to the stocking.

Spindler gave a weak laugh. "Well, you see, ef it comes to that, I've never seen 'em!"

Mrs. Price put the stocking in her lap and opened her direct eyes on Spindler. "Never seen 'em?" she repeated. "Then, they're not near relations?"

"There are three cousins," said Spindler, checking them off on his fingers, "a half-uncle, a kind of brother-in-law,--that is, the brother of my sister-in-law's second husband,--and a niece. That's six."

"But if you've not seen them, I suppose they've corresponded with you?" said Mrs. Price.

"They've nearly all of 'em written to me for money, seeing my name in the paper ez hevin' made a strike," returned Spindler simply; "and hevin' sent it, I jest know their addresses."

"Oh!" said Mrs. Price, returning to the stocking.

Something in the tone of her ejaculation increased Spindler's embarrassment, but it also made him desperate. "You see, Mrs. Price," he blurted out, "I oughter tell ye that I reckon they are the folks that 'hevn't got on,' don't you see, and so it seemed only the square thing for me, ez had 'got on,' to give them a sort o' Christmas festival. Suthin', don't ye know, like what your brother-in-law was sayin' last Sunday in the pulpit about this yer peace and goodwill 'twixt man and man."

Mrs. Price looked again at the man before her. His sallow, perplexed face exhibited some doubt, yet a certain determination, regarding the prospect the quotation had opened to him. "A very good idea, Mr. Spindler, and one that does you great credit," she said gravely.

"I'm mighty glad to hear you say so, Mrs. Price," he said, with an accent of great relief, "for I reckoned to ask you a great favor! You see," he fell into his former hesitation, "that is--the fact is--that this sort o' thing is rather suddent to me,--a little outer my line, don't you see, and I was goin' to ask ye ef you'd mind takin' the hull thing in hand and runnin it for me."

"Running it for you," said Mrs. Price, with a quick eye-shot from under the edge of her lashes. "Man alive! What are you thinking of?"

"Bossin' the whole job for me," hurried on Spindler, with nervous desperation. "Gettin' together all the things and makin' ready for 'em,--orderin' in everythin' that's wanted, and fixin' up the rooms,--I kin step out while you're doin' it,--and then helpin' me receivin' 'em, and sittin' at the head o' the table, you know,--like ez ef you was the mistress."

"But," said Mrs. Price, with her frank laugh, "that's the duty of one of your relations,--your niece, for instance,--or cousin, if one of them is a woman."

"But," persisted Spindler, "you see, they're strangers to me; I don't know 'em, and I do you. You'd make it easy for 'em,--and for me,--don't you see? Kinder introduce 'em,--don't you know? A woman of your gin'ral experience would smooth down all them little difficulties," continued Spindler, with a vague recollection of the Kansas story, "and put everybody on velvet. Don't say 'No,' Mrs. Price! I'm just kalkilatin' on you."

Sincerity and persistency in a man goes a great way with even the best of women. Mrs. Price, who had at first received Spindler's request as an amusing originality, now began to incline secretly towards it. And, of course, began to suggest objections.

"I'm afraid it won't do," she said thoughtfully, awakening to the fact that it would do and could be done. "You see, I've promised to spend Christmas at Sacramento with my nieces from Baltimore. And then there's Mrs. Saltover and my sister to consult."

But here Spindler's simple face showed such signs of distress that the widow declared she would "think it over,"--a process which the sanguine Spindler seemed to consider so nearly akin to talking it over that Mrs. Price began to believe it herself, as he hopefully departed.

She "thought it over" sufficiently to go to Sacramento and excuse herself to her nieces. But here she permitted herself to "talk it over," to the infinite delight of those Baltimore girls, who thought this extravaganza of Spindler's "so Californian and eccentric!" So that it was not strange that presently the news came back to Rough and Ready, and his old associates learned for the first time that he had never seen his relatives, and that they would be doubly strangers. This did not increase his popularity; neither, I grieve to say, did the intelligence that his relatives were probably poor, and that the Reverend Mr. Saltover had approved of his course, and had likened it to the rich man's feast, to which the halt and blind were invited. Indeed, the allusion was supposed to add hypocrisy and a bid for popularity to Spindler's defection, for it was argued that he might have feasted "Wall-eyed Joe" or "Tanglefoot Billy,"--who had once been "chawed" by a bear while prospecting,--if he had been sincere. Howbeit, Spindler's faith was oblivious to these criticisms, in his joy at Mr. Saltover's adhesion to his plans and the loan of Mrs. Price as a hostess. In fact, he proposed to her that the invitation should also convey that information in the expression, "by the kind permission of the Rev. Mr. Saltover," as a guarantee of good faith, but the widow would have none of it. The invitations were duly written and dispatched.

"Suppose," suggested Spindler, with a sudden lugubrious apprehension,--"suppose they shouldn't come?"

"Have no fear of that," said Mrs. Price, with a frank laugh.

"Or ef they was dead," continued Spindler.

"They couldn't all be dead," said the widow cheerfully.

"I've written to another cousin by marriage," said Spindler dubiously, "in case of accident; I didn't think of him before, because he was rich."

"And have you ever seen him either, Mr. Spindler?" asked the widow, with a slight mischievousness.

"Lordy! No!" he responded, with unaffected concern.

Only one mistake was made by Mrs. Price in her arrangements for the party. She had noticed what the simple-minded Spindler could never have conceived,--the feeling towards him held by his old associates, and had tactfully suggested that a general invitation should be extended to them in the evening.

"You can have refreshments, you know, too, after the dinner, and games and music."

"But," said the unsophisticated host, "won't the boys think I'm playing it rather low down on them, so to speak, givin' 'em a kind o' second table, as ef it was the tailings after a strike?"

"Nonsense," said Mrs. Price, with decision. "It's quite fashionable in San Francisco, and just the thing to do."

To this decision Spindler, in his blind faith in the widow's management, weakly yielded. An announcement in the "Weekly Banner" that, "On Christmas evening Richard Spindler, Esq., proposed to entertain his friends and fellow citizens at an 'at home,' in his own residence," not only widened the breach between him and the "boys," but awakened an active resentment that only waited for an outlet. It was understood that they were all coming; but that they should have "some fun out of it" which might not coincide with Spindler's nor his relatives' sense of humor seemed a foregone conclusion.

Unfortunately, too, subsequent events lent themselves to this irony of the situation. He was so obviously sincere in his intent, and, above all, seemed to place such a pathetic reliance on her judgment, that she hesitated to let him know the shock his revelation had given her. And what might his other relations prove to be? Good Lord! Yet, oddly enough, she was so prepossessed by him, and so fascinated by his very Quixotism, that it was perhaps for these complex reasons that she said a little stiffly:--

"One of these cousins, I see, is a lady, and then there is your niece. Do you know anything about them, Mr. Spindler?"

His face grew serious. "No more than I know of the others," he said apologetically. After a moment's hesitation he went on: "Now you speak of it, it seems to me I've heard that my niece was di-vorced. But," he added, brightening up, "I've heard that she was popular."

Mrs. Price gave a short laugh, and was silent for a few minutes. Then this sublime little woman looked up at him. What he might have seen in her eyes was more than he expected, or, I fear, deserved. "Cheer up, Mr. Spindler," she said manfully. "I'll see you through this thing, don't you mind! But don't you say anything about--about--this Vigilance Committee business to anybody. Nor about your niece--it was your niece, wasn't it?--being divorced. Charley (the late Mr. Price) had a queer sort of sister, who--but that's neither here nor there! And your niece mayn't come, you know; or if she does, you ain't bound to bring her out to the general company."

At parting, Spindler, in sheer gratefulness, pressed her hand, and lingered so long over it that a little color sprang into the widow's brown cheek. Perhaps a fresh courage sprang into her heart, too, for she went to Sacramento the next day, previously enjoining Spindler on no account to show any answers he might receive. At Sacramento her nieces flew to her with confidences.

"We so wanted to see you, Aunt Huldy, for we've heard something so delightful about your funny Christmas Party!" Mrs. Price's heart sank, but her eyes snapped. "Only think of it! One of Mr. Spindler's long-lost relatives--a Mr. Wragg--lives in this hotel, and papa knows him. He's a sort of half-uncle, I believe, and he's just furious that Spindler should have invited him. He showed papa the letter; said it was the greatest piece of insolence in the world; that Spindler was an ostentatious fool, who had made a little money and wanted to use him to get into society; and the fun of the whole thing was that this half-uncle and whole brute is himself a parvenu,--a vulgar, ostentatious creature, who was only a"--

"Never mind what he was, Kate," interrupted Mrs. Price hastily. "I call his conduct a shame."

"So do we," said both girls eagerly. After a pause Kate clasped her knees with her locked fingers, and rocking backwards and forwards, said, "Milly and I have got an idea, and don't you say 'No' to it. We've had it ever since that brute talked in that way. Now, through him, we know more about this Mr. Spindler's family connections than you do; and we know all the trouble you and he'll have in getting up this party. You understand? Now, we first want to know what Spindler's like. Is he a savage, bearded creature, like the miners we saw on the boat?"

Mrs. Price said that, on the contrary, he was very gentle, soft-spoken, and rather good-looking.

"Young or old?"

"Young,--in fact, a mere boy, as you may judge from his actions," returned Mrs. Price, with a suggestive matronly air.

Kate here put up a long-handled eyeglass to her fine gray eyes, fitted it ostentatiously over her aquiline nose, and then said, in a voice of simulated horror, "Aunt Huldy,--this revelation is shocking!"

Mrs. Price laughed her usual frank laugh, albeit her brown cheek took upon it a faint tint of Indian red. "If that's the wonderful idea you girls have got, I don't see how it's going to help matters," she said dryly.

"No, that's not it? We really have an idea. Now look here."

Mrs. Price "looked here." This process seemed to the superficial observer to be merely submitting her waist and shoulders to the arms of her nieces, and her ears to their confidential and coaxing voices.

Twice she said "it couldn't be thought of," and "it was impossible;" once addressed Kate as "You limb!" and finally said that she "wouldn't promise, but might write!"

It was two days before Christmas. There was nothing in the air, sky, or landscape of that Sierran slope to suggest the season to the Eastern stranger. A soft rain had been dropping for a week on laurel, pine, and buckeye, and the blades of springing grasses and shyly opening flowers. Sedate and silent hillsides that had grown dumb and parched towards the end of the dry season became gently articulate again; there were murmurs in hushed and forgotten canyons, the leap and laugh of water among the dry bones of dusty creeks, and the full song of the larger forks and rivers. Southwest winds brought the warm odor of the pine sap swelling in the forest, or the faint, far-off spice of wild mustard springing in the lower valleys. But, as if by some irony of Nature, this gentle invasion of spring in the wild wood brought only disturbance and discomfort to the haunts and works of man. The ditches were overflowed, the fords of the Fork impassable, the sluicing adrift, and the trails and wagon roads to Rough and Ready knee-deep in mud. The stage-coach from Sacramento, entering the settlement by the mountain highway, its wheels and panels clogged and crusted with an unctuous pigment like mud and blood, passed out of it through the overflowed and dangerous ford, and emerged in spotless purity, leaving its stains behind with Rough and Ready. A week of enforced idleness on the river "Bar" had driven the miners to the more comfortable recreation of the saloon bar, its mirrors, its florid paintings, its armchairs, and its stove. The steam of their wet boots and the smoke of their pipes hung over the latter like the sacrificial incense from an altar. But the attitude of the men was more critical and censorious than contented, and showed little of the gentleness of the weather or season.

"Did you hear if the stage brought down any more relations of Spindler's?"

The barkeeper, to whom this question was addressed, shifted his lounging position against the bar and said, "I reckon not, ez far ez I know."

"And that old bloat of a second cousin--that crimson beak--what kem down yesterday,--he ain't bin hangin' round here today for his reg'lar pizon?"

"No," said the barkeeper thoughtfully, "I reckon Spindler's got him locked up, and is settin' on him to keep him sober till after Christmas, and prevent you boys gettin' at him."

"He'll have the jimjams before that," returned the first speaker; "and how about that dead beat of a half-nephew who borrowed twenty dollars of Yuba Bill on the way down, and then wanted to get off at Shootersvilie, but Bill wouldn't let him, and scooted him down to Spindler's and collected the money from Spindler himself afore he'd give him up?"

"He's up thar with the rest of the menagerie," said the barkeeper, "but I reckon that Mrs. Price hez bin feedin' him up. And ye know the old woman--that fifty-fifth cousin by marriage--whom Joe Chandler swears he remembers ez an old cook for a Chinese restaurant in Stockton,--darn my skin ef that Mrs. Price hasn't rigged her out in some fancy duds of her own, and made her look quite decent."

A deep groan here broke from Uncle Jim Starbuck.

"Didn't I tell ye?" he said, turning appealingly to the others. "It's that darned widow that's at the bottom of it all! She first put Spindler up to givin' the party, and now, darn my skin, ef she ain't goin to fix up these ragamuffins and drill 'em so we can't get any fun outer 'em after all! And it's bein' a woman that's bossin' the job, and not Spindler, we've got to draw things mighty fine and not cut up too rough, or some of the boys will kick."

"You bet," said a surly but decided voice in the crowd.

"And," said another voice, "Mrs. Price didn't live in 'Bleeding Kansas' for nothing."

"Wot's the programme you've settled on, Uncle Jim?" said the barkeeper lightly, to check what seemed to promise a dangerous discussion.

"Well," said Starbuck, "we kalkilate to gather early Christmas night in Hooper's Hollow and rig ourselves up Injun fashion, and then start for Spindler's with pitch-pine torches, and have a 'torchlight dance' around the house; them who does the dancin' and yellin' outside takin' their turn at goin' in and hevin' refreshment. Jake Cooledge, of Boston, sez if anybody objects to it, we've only got to say we're 'Mummers of the Olden Times,' sabe? Then, later, we'll have 'Them Sabbath Evening Bells' performed on prospectin' pans by the band. Then, at the finish, Jake Cooledge is goin' to give one of his surkastic speeches,--kinder welcomin' Spindler's family to the Free Openin' o' Spindler's Almshouse and Reformatory." He paused, possibly for that approbation which, however, did not seem to come spontaneously. "It ain't much," he added apologetically, "for we're hampered by women; but we'll add to the programme ez we see how things pan out. Ye see, from what we can hear, all of Spindler's relations ain't on hand yet! We've got to wait, like in elckshun times, for 'returns from the back counties.' Hello! What's that?"

It was the swish and splutter of hoofs on the road before the door. The Sacramento coach! In an instant every man was expectant, and Starbuck darted outside on the platform. Then there was the usual greeting and bustle, the hurried ingress of thirsty passengers into the saloon, and a pause. Uncle Jim returned, excitedly and pantingly. "Look yer, boys! Ef this ain't the richest thing out! They say there's two more relations o' Spindler's on the coach, come down as express freight, consigned,--d'ye hear?--consigned to Spindler!"

"Stiffs, in coffins?" suggested an eager voice.

"I didn't get to hear more. But here they are."

There was the sudden irruption of a laughing, curious crowd into the barroom, led by Yuba Bill, the driver. Then the crowd parted, and out of their midst stepped two children, a boy and a girl, the oldest apparently of not more than six years, holding each other's hands. They were coarsely yet cleanly dressed, and with a certain uniform precision that suggested formal charity. But more remarkable than all, around the neck of each was a little steel chain, from which depended the regular check and label of the powerful Express Company, Wells; Fargo & Co., and the words: "To Richard Spindler." "Fragile." "With great care." "Collect on delivery." Occasionally their little hands went up automatically and touched their labels, as if to show them. They surveyed the crowd, the floor, the gilded bar, and Yuba Bill without fear and without wonder. There was a pathetic suggestion that they were accustomed to this observation.

"Now, Bobby," said Yuba Bill, leaning back against the bar, with an air half-paternal, half-managerial, "tell these gents how you came here."

"By Wellth, Fargoth Expreth," lisped Bobby.

"Whar from?"

"Wed Hill, Owegon."

"Red Hill, Oregon? Why, it's a thousand miles from here," said a bystander.

"I reckon," said Yuba Bill coolly, "they kem by stage to Portland, by steamer to 'Frisco, steamer again to Stockton, and then by stage over the whole line. Allers by Wells, Fargo & Co.'s Express, from agent to agent, and from messenger to messenger. Fact! They ain't bin tetched or handled by any one but the Kempany's agents; they ain't had a line or direction except them checks around their necks! And they've wanted for nothin' else. Why, I've carried heaps o' treasure before, gentlemen, and once a hundred thousand dollars in greenbacks, but I never carried anythin' that was watched and guarded as them kids! Why, the division inspector at Stockton wanted to go with 'em over the line; but Jim Bracy, the messenger, said he'd call it a reflection on himself and resign, ef they didn't give 'em to him with the other packages! Ye had a pretty good time, Bobby, didn't ye? Plenty to eat and drink, eh?"

The two children laughed a little weak laugh, turned each other bashfully around, and then looked up shyly at Yuba Bill and said, "Yeth."

"Do you know where you are goin'?" asked Starbuck, in a constrained voice.

It was the little girl who answered quickly and eagerly:--

"Yes, to Krissmass and Sandy Claus."

"To what?" asked Starbuck.

Here the boy interposed with a superior air:--

"Thee meanth Couthin Dick. He'th got Krithmath."

"Where's your mother?"

"Dead."

"And your father?"

"In orthpittal."

There was a laugh somewhere on the outskirts of the crowd. Every one faced angrily in that direction, but the laugher had disappeared. Yuba Bill, however, sent his voice after him. "Yes, in hospital! Funny, ain't it?--amoosin' place! Try it. Step over here, and in five minutes, by the living Hoky, I'll qualify you for admission, and not charge you a cent!" He stopped, gave a sweeping glance of dissatisfaction around him, and then, leaning back against the bar, beckoned to some one near the door, and said in a disgusted tone, "You tell these galoots how it happened, Bracy. They make me sick!"

Thus appealed to, Bracy, the express messenger, stepped forward in Yuba Bill's place.

"It's nothing particular, gentlemen," he said, with a laugh, "only it seems that some man called Spindler, who lives about here, sent an invitation to the father of these children to bring his family to a Christmas party. It wasn't a bad sort of thing for Spindler to do, considering that they were his poor relations, though they didn't know him from Adam,--was it?" He paused; several of the bystanders cleared their throats, but said nothing. "At least," resumed Bracy, "that's what the boys up at

Red Hill, Oregon, thought, when they heard of it. Well, as the father was in hospital with a broken leg, and the mother only a few weeks dead, the boys thought it mighty rough on these poor kids if they were done out of their fun because they had no one to bring them. The boys couldn't afford to go themselves, but they got a little money together, and then got the idea of sendin' 'em by express. Our agent at Red Hill tumbled to the idea at once; but he wouldn't take any money in advance, and said he would send 'em 'C. O. D.' like any other package. And he did, and here they are! That's all! And now, gentlemen, as I've got to deliver them personally to this Spindler, and get his receipt and take off their checks, I reckon we must toddle. Come, Bill, help take 'em up!"

"Hold on!" said a dozen voices. A dozen hands were thrust into a dozen pockets; I grieve to say some were regretfully withdrawn empty, for it was a hard season in Rough and Ready. But the expressman stepped before them, with warning, uplifted hand.

"Not a cent, boys,--not a cent! Wells, Fargo's Express Company don't undertake to carry bullion with those kids, at least on the same contract!" He laughed, and then looking around him, said confidentially in a lower voice, which, however, was quite audible to the children, "There's as much as three bags of silver in quarter and half dollars in my treasure box in the coach that has been poured, yes, just showered upon them, ever since they started, and have been passed over from agent to agent and messenger to messenger,--enough to pay their passage from here to China! It's time to say quits now. But bet your life, they are not going to that Christmas party poor!"

He caught up the boy, as Yuba Bill lifted the little girl to his shoulder, and both passed out. Then one by one the loungers in the bar-room silently and awkwardly followed, and when the barkeeper turned back from putting away his decanters and glasses, to his astonishment the room was empty.

*****

Spindler's house, or "Spindler's Splurge," as Rough and Ready chose to call it, stood above the settlement, on a deforested hillside, which, however, revenged itself by producing not enough vegetation to cover even the few stumps that were ineradicable. A large wooden structure in the pseudo-classic style affected by Westerners, with an incongruous cupola, it was oddly enough relieved by a still more incongruous veranda extending around its four sides, upheld by wooden Doric columns, which were already picturesquely covered with flowering vines and sun-loving roses. Mr. Spindler had trusted the furnishing of its interior to the same contractor who had upholstered the gilded bar-room of the Eureka Saloon, and who had apparently bestowed the same design and material, impartially, on each. There were gilded mirrors all over the house and chilly marble-topped tables, gilt plaster Cupids in the corners, and stuccoed lions "in the way" everywhere. The tactful hands of Mrs. Price had screened some of these with seasonable laurels, fir boughs, and berries, and had imparted a slight Christmas flavor to the house. But the greater part of her time had been employed in trying to subdue the eccentricities of Spindler's amazing relations; in tranquilizing Mrs. "Aunt" Martha Spindler,-- the elderly cook before alluded to,--who was inclined to regard the gilded splendors of the house as indicative of dangerous immorality; in restraining "Cousin" Morley Hewlett from considering the dining-room buffet as a bar for "intermittent refreshment;" and in keeping the weak-minded nephew, Phinney Spindler, from shooting at bottles from the veranda, wearing his uncle's clothes, or running up an account in his uncle's name for various articles at the general stores. Yet the unlooked-for arrival of the two children had been the one great compensation and diversion for her. She wrote at once to her nieces a brief account of her miraculous deliverance. "I think these poor children dropped from the skies here to make our Christmas party possible, to say nothing of the sympathy they have created in Rough and Ready for Spindler. He is going to keep them as long as he can, and is writing to the father. Think of the poor little tots traveling a thousand miles to 'Krissmass,' as they call it!--though they were so well cared for by the messengers that their little bodies were positively stuffed like quails. So, you see, dear, we will be able to get along without airing your famous idea. I'm sorry, for I know you're just dying to see it all."

Whatever Kate's "idea" might have been, there certainly seemed now no need of any extraneous aid to Mrs. Price's management. Christmas came at last, and the dinner passed off without serious disaster. But the ordeal of the reception of Rough and Ready was still to come. For Mrs. Price well knew that although "the boys" were more subdued, and, indeed, inclined to sympathize with their host's uncouth endeavor, there was still much in the aspect of Spindler's relations to excite their sense of the ludicrous. But here Fortune again favored the house of Spindler with a dramatic surprise, even greater than the advent of the children had been. In the change that had come over Rough and Ready, "the boys" had decided, out of deference to the women and children, to omit the first part of their programme, and had approached and entered the house as soberly and quietly as ordinary guests. But before they had shaken hands with the host and hostess, and seen the relations, the clatter of wheels was heard before the open door, and its lights flashed upon a carriage and pair,--an actual private carriage,--the like of which had not been seen since the governor of the State had come down to open the new ditch! Then there was a pause, the flash of the carriage lamps upon white silk, the light tread of a satin foot on the veranda and in the hall, and the entrance of a vision of loveliness! Middle-aged men and old dwellers of cities remembered their youth; younger men bethought themselves of Cinderella and the Prince! There was a thrill and a hush as this last guest--a beautiful girl, radiant with youth and adornment--put a dainty glass to her sparkling eye and advanced familiarly, with outstretched hand, to Dick Spindler. Mrs. Price gave a single gasp, and drew back speechless.

"Uncle Dick," said a laughing contralto voice, which, indeed, somewhat recalled Mrs. Price's own, in its courageous frankness, "I am so delighted to come, even if a little late, and so sorry that Mr. M'Kenna could not come on account of business."

Everybody listened eagerly, but none more eagerly and surprisingly than the host himself. M'Kenna! The rich cousin who had never answered the invitation! And Uncle Dick! This, then, was his divorced niece! Yet even in his astonishment he remembered that of course no one but himself and Mrs. Price knew it,--and that lady had glanced discreetly away.

"Yes," continued the half-niece brightly. "I came from Sacramento with some friends to Shootersville, and from thence I drove here; and though I must return to-night, I could not forego the pleasure of coming, if it was only for an hour or two, to answer the invitation of the uncle I have not seen for years." She paused, and, raising her glasses, turned a politely questioning eye towards Mrs. Price. "One of our relations?" she said smilingly to Spindler.

"No," said Spindler, with some embarrassment, "a--a friend!"

The half-niece extended her hand. Mrs. Price took it.

But the fair stranger,--what she did and said were the only things remembered in Rough and Ready on that festive occasion; no one thought of the other relations; no one recalled them nor their eccentricities; Spindler himself was forgotten. People only recollected how Spindler's lovely niece lavished her smiles and courtesies on every one, and brought to her feet particularly the misogynist Starbuck and the sarcastic Cooledge, oblivious of his previous speech; how she sat at the piano and sang like an angel, hushing the most hilarious and excited into sentimental and even maudlin silence; how, graceful as a nymph, she led with "Uncle Dick" a Virginia reel until the whole assembly joined, eager for a passing touch of her dainty hand in its changes; how, when two hours had passed,--all too swiftly for the guests,--they stood with bared heads and glistening eyes on the veranda to see the fairy coach whirl the fairy princess away! How--but this incident was never known to Rough and Ready. It happened in the sacred dressing-room, where Mrs. Price was cloaking with her own hands the departing half-niece of Mr. Spindler. Taking that opportunity to seize the lovely relative by the shoulders and shake her violently, she said: "Oh, yes, and it's all very well for you, Kate, you limb! For you're going away, and will never see Rough and Ready and poor Spindler again. But what am I to do, miss? How am I to face it out? For you know I've got to tell him at least that you're no half-niece of his!"

"Have you?" said the young lady.

"Have I?" repeated the widow impatiently. "Have I? Of course I have! What are you thinking of?"

"I was thinking, aunty," said the girl audaciously, "that from what I've seen and heard to-night, if I'm not his half-niece now, it's only a question of time! So you'd better wait. Good-night, dear."

And, really,--it turned out that she was right!

WHEN THE WATERS WERE UP AT "JULES'"

When the waters were up at "Jules'" there was little else up on that monotonous level. For the few inhabitants who calmly and methodically moved to higher ground, camping out in tents until the flood had subsided, left no distracting wreckage behind them. A dozen half-submerged log cabins dotted the tranquil surface of the waters, without ripple or disturbance, looking in the moonlight more like the ruins of centuries than of a few days. There was no current to sap their slight foundations or sweep them away; nothing stirred that silent lake but the occasional shot-like indentations of a passing raindrop, or, still more rarely, a raft, made of a single log, propelled by some citizen on a tour of inspection of his cabin roof-tree, where some of his goods were still stored. There was no sense of terror in this bland obliteration of the little settlement; the ruins of a single burnt-up cabin would have been more impressive than this stupid and even grotesquely placid effect of the rival destroying element. People took it naturally; the water went as it had come,--slowly, impassively, noiselessly; a few days of fervid Californian sunshine dried the cabins, and in a week or two the red dust lay again as thickly before their doors as the winter mud had lain. The waters of Rattlesnake Creek dropped below its banks, the stage-coach from Marysville no longer made a detour of the settlement. There was even a singular compensation to this amicable invasion; the inhabitants sometimes found gold in those breaches in the banks made by the overflow. To wait for the "old Rattlesnake sluicing" was a vernal hope of the trusting miner.

The history of "Jules'," however, was once destined to offer a singular interruption of this peaceful and methodical process. The winter of 1859-60 was an exceptional one. But little rain had fallen in the valleys, although the snow lay deep in the high Sierras. Passes were choked, ravines filled, and glaciers found on their slopes.

And when the tardy rains came with the withheld southwesterly "trades," the regular phenomenon recurred; Jules' Flat silently, noiselessly, and peacefully went under water; the inhabitants moved to the higher ground, perhaps a little more expeditiously from an impatience born of the delay. The stagecoach from Marysville made its usual detour and stopped before the temporary hotel, express offices, and general store of "Jules'," under canvas, bark, and the limp leaves of a spreading alder. It deposited a single passenger,--Miles Hemmingway, of San Francisco, but originally of Boston,--the young secretary of a mining company, dispatched to report upon the alleged auriferous value of "Jules'." Of this he had been by no means impressed as he looked down upon the submerged cabins from the box-seat of the coach and listened to the driver's lazy recital of the flood, and of the singularly patient acceptance of it by the inhabitants.

It was the old story of the southwestern miner's indolence and incompetency,--utterly distasteful to his northern habits of thought and education. Here was their old fatuous endurance of Nature's wild caprices, without that struggle against them which brought others strength and success; here was the old philosophy which accepted the prairie fire and cyclone, and survived them without advancement, yet without repining. Perhaps in different places and surroundings a submission so stoic might have impressed him; in gentlemen who tucked their dirty trousers in their muddy boots and lived only for the gold they dug, it did not seem to him heroic. Nor was he mollified as he stood beside the rude refreshment bar--a few planks laid on trestles--and drank his coffee beneath the dripping canvas roof, with an odd recollection of his boyhood and an inclement Sunday-school picnic. Yet these men had been living in this shiftless fashion for three weeks! It exasperated him still more to think that he might have to wait there a few days longer for the water to subside sufficiently for him to make his examination and report. As he took a proffered seat on a candle-box, which tilted under him, and another survey of the feeble makeshifts around him, his irascibility found vent.

"Why, in the name of God, didn't you, after you had been flooded out ONCE, build your cabins PERMANENTLY on higher ground?"

Although the tone of his voice was more disturbing than his question, it pleased one of the loungers to affect to take it literally.

"Well, ez you've put it that way,--'in the name of God!'"--returned the man lazily, "it mout hev struck us that ez HE was bossin' the job, so to speak, and hand-lin' things round here generally, we might leave it to Him. It wasn't OUR flood to monkey with."

"And as He didn't coven-ant, so to speak, to look arter this higher ground 'spe-shally, and make an Ararat of it for us, ez far ez we could see, we didn't see any reason for SETTLIN' yer," put in a second speaker, with equal laziness.

The secretary saw his mistake instantly, and had experience enough of Western humor not to prolong the disadvantage of his unfortunate adjuration. He colored slightly and said, with a smile, "You know what I mean; you could have protected yourselves better. A levee on the bank would have kept you clear of the highest watermark."

"Hey you ever heard WHAT the highest watermark was?" said the first speak-er, turning to another of the loungers without looking at the secretary.

"Never heard it,--didn't know there was a limit before," responded the man.

The first speaker turned back to the secretary. "Did you ever know what hap-pened at 'Bulger's,' on the North Fork? They had one o' them levees."

"No. What happened?" asked the secretary impatiently.

"They was fixed suthin' like us," returned the first speaker. "THEY allowed they'd build a levee above THEIR highest watermark, and did. It worked like a charm at first; but the water hed to go somewhere, and it kinder collected at the first bend. Then it sorter raised itself on its elbows one day, and looked over the levee down upon whar some of the boys was washin' quite comf'ble. Then it paid no sorter attention to the limit o' that high watermark, but went six inches better! Not slow and quiet like ez it useter to, ez it does HERE, kinder fillin' up from below, but went over with a rush and a current, hevin' of course the whole height of the levee to fall on t'other side where the boys were sluicing." He paused, and amidst a profound silence added, "They say that 'Bulger's' was scattered promiscuous-like all along the fort for five miles. I only know that one of his mules and a section of sluicing was picked up at Red Flat, eight miles away!"

Mr. Hemmingway felt that there WAS an answer to this, but, being wise, also felt that it would be unavailing. He smiled politely and said nothing, at which the first speaker turned to him:--

"Thar ain't anything to see to-day, but to-morrow, ez things go, the water oughter be droppin'. Mebbe you'd like to wash up now and clean yourself," he added, with a glance at Hemmingway's small portmanteau. "Ez we thought you'd likely be crowded here, we've rigged up a corner for you at Stanton's shanty with the women."

The young man's cheek flushed slightly at some possible irony in this, and he protested with considerable stress that he was quite ready "to rough it" where he was.

"I reckon it's already fixed," returned the man decisively, "so you'd better come and I'll show you the way."

"One moment," said Hemmingway, with a smile; "my credentials are addressed to the manager of the Boone Ditch Company at 'Jules'.' Perhaps I ought to see him first."

"All right; he's Stanton."

"And"--hesitated the secretary, "YOU, who appear to understand the locality so well,--I trust I may have the pleasure"--

"Oh, I'm Jules."

The secretary was a little startled and amused. So "Jules" was a person, and not a place!

"Then you're a pioneer?" asked Hemmingway, a little less dictatorially, as they passed out under the dripping trees.

"I struck this creek in the fall of '49, comin' over Livermore's Pass with Stanton," returned Jules, with great brevity of speech and deliberate tardiness of delivery. "Sent for my wife and two children the next year; wife died same winter, change bein' too sudden for her, and contractin' chills and fever at Sweetwater. When I kem here first thar wasn't six inches o' water in the creek; out there was a heap of it over there where you see them yellowish-green patches and strips o' brush and grass; all that war water then, and all that growth hez sprung up since."

Hemmingway looked around him. The "higher ground" where they stood was in reality only a mound-like elevation above the dead level of the flat, and the few trees were merely recent young willows and alders. The area of actual depression was much greater than he had imagined, and its resemblance to the bed of some prehistoric inland sea struck him forcibly. A previous larger inundation than Jules' brief experience had ever known had been by no means improbable. His cheek reddened at his previous hasty indictment of the settlers' ignorance and shiftlessness, and the thought that he had probably committed his employers to his own rash confidence and superiority of judgment. However, there was no evidence that this diluvial record was not of the remote past. He smiled again with greater security as he thought of the geological changes that had since tempered these cataclysms, and the amelioration brought by settlement and cultivation. Nevertheless, he would make a thorough examination to-morrow.

Stanton's cabin was the furthest of these temporary habitations, and was partly on the declivity which began to slope to the river's bank. It was, like the others, a rough shanty of unplaned boards, but, unlike the others, it had a base of logs laid lengthwise on the ground and parallel with each other, on which the flooring and structure were securely fastened. This gave it the appearance of a box slid on runners, or a Noah's Ark whose bulk had been reduced. Jules explained that the logs, laid in that manner, kept the shanty warmer and free from damp. In reply to Hemmingway's suggestion that it was a great waste of material, Jules simply replied that the logs were the "flotsam and jetsam" of the creek from the overflowed mills below.

Hemmingway again smiled. It was again the old story of Western waste and prodigality. Accompanied by Jules, however, he climbed up the huge, slippery logs which made a platform before the door, and entered.

The single room was unequally divided; the larger part containing three beds, by day rolled in a single pile in one corner to make room for a table and chairs. A few dresses hanging from nails on the wall showed that it was the women's room. The smaller compartment was again subdivided by a hanging blanket, behind which was a rude bunk or berth against the wall, a table made of a packing-box, containing a tin basin and a can of water. This was his apartment.

"The women-folks are down the creek, bakin', to-day," said Jules explanatorily; "but I reckon that one of 'em will be up here in a jiffy to make supper, so you just take it easy till they come. I've got to meander over to the claim afore I turn in, but you just lie by to-night and take a rest."

He turned away, leaving Hemmingway standing in the doorway still distraught and hesitating. Nor did the young man recognize the delicacy of Jules' leave-taking until he had unstrapped his portmanteau and found himself alone, free to make his toilet, unembarrassed by company. But even then he would have preferred the rough companionship of the miners in the common dormitory of the general store to this intrusion upon the half-civilization of the women, their pitiable little comforts and secret makeshifts. His disgust of his own indecision which brought him there naturally recoiled in the direction of his host and hostesses, and after a hurried ablution, a change of linen, and an attempt to remove the stains of travel from his clothes, he strode out impatiently into the open air again.

It was singularly mild even for the season. The southwest trades blew softly, and whispered to him of San Francisco and the distant Pacific, with its long, steady swell. He turned again to the overflowed Flat beneath him, and the sluggish yellow water that scarcely broke a ripple against the walls of the half-submerged cabins. And this was the water for whose going down they were waiting with an immobility as tranquil as the waters themselves! What marvelous incompetency,--or what infinite patience! He knew, of course, their expected compensation in this "ground sluicing" at Nature's own hand; the long rifts in the banks of the creek which so often showed "the color" in the sparkling scales of river gold disclosed by the action of the water; the heaps of reddish mud left after its subsidence around the walls of the cabins,--a deposit that often contained a treasure a dozen times more valuable than the cabin itself! And then he heard behind him a laugh, a short and panting breath, and turning, beheld a young woman running towards him.

In his first astounded sight of her, in her limp nankeen sunbonnet, thrown back from her head by the impetus of her flight, he saw only too much hair, two much white teeth, too much eye-flash, and, above all,--as it appeared to him,--too much confidence in the power of these qualities. Even as she ran, it seemed to him that she was pulling down ostentatiously the rolled-up sleeves of her pink calico gown over her shapely arms. I am inclined to think that the young gentleman's temper was at fault, and his conclusion hasty; a calmer observer would have detected nothing of this in her frankly cheerful voice. Nevertheless, her evident pleasure in the meeting seemed to him only obtrusive coquetry.

"Lordy! I reckoned to git here afore you'd get through fixin' up, and in time to do a little prinkin' myself, and here you're out already." She laughed, glancing at his clean shirt and damp hair. "But all the same, we kin have a talk, and you kin tell me all the news afore the other wimmen get up here. It's a coon's age since I was at

Sacramento and saw anybody or anything." She stopped and, instinctively detecting some vague reticence in the man before her, said, still laughing, "You're Mr. Hemmingway, ain't you?"

Hemmingway took off his hat quickly, with a slight start at his forgetfulness. "I beg your pardon; yes, certainly."

"Aunty Stanton thought it was 'Hummingbird,'" said the girl, with a laugh, "but I reckoned not. I'm Jinney Jules, you know; folks call me 'J. J.' It wouldn't do for a Hummingbird and a Jay Jay to be in the same camp, would it? It would be just TOO funny!"

Hemmingway did not find the humor of this so singularly exhaustive, but he was already beginning to be ashamed of his attitude towards her. "I'm very sorry to be giving you all this trouble by my intrusion, for I was quite willing to stay at the store yonder. Indeed," he added, with a burst of frankness quite as sincere as her own, "if you think your father will not be offended, I would gladly go there now."

If he still believed in her coquetry and vanity, he would have been undeceived and crushed by the equal and sincere frankness with which she met this ungallant speech.

"No! I reckon he wouldn't care, if you'd be as comf'ble and fit for to-morrow. But ye WOULDN'T," she said reflectively. "The boys thar sit up late over euchre, and swear a heap, and Simpson, who'd sleep alongside of ye, snores pow'ful, I've heard. Aunty Stanton kin do her level at that, too, and they say"--with a laugh--"that I kin, too, but you're away off in that corner, and it won't reach you. So, takin' it all, by the large, you'd better stay whar ye are. We wimmen, that is, the most of us, will be off and away down to Rattlesnake Bar shoppin' afore sun up, so ye'll sleep ez long ez ye want to, and find yer breakfast ready when ye wake. So I'll jest set to and get ye some supper, and ye kin tell me all the doin's in Sacramento and 'Frisco while I'm workin'."

In spite of her unconscious rebuff to his own vanity, Hemmingway felt a sense of relief and less constraint in his relations to this decidedly provincial hostess.

"Can I help you in any way?" he asked eagerly.

"Well, ye MIGHT bring me an armful o' wood from the pile under the alders, ef ye ain't afraid o' dirtyin' your coat," she said tentatively.

Mr. Hemmingway was not afraid; he declared himself delighted. He brought a generous armful of small cut willow boughs, and deposited them before a small stove, which seemed a temporary substitute for the usual large adobe chimney that generally occupied the entire gable of a miner's cabin. An elbow and short length of stovepipe carried the smoke through the cabin side. But he also noticed that his fair companion had used the interval to put on a pair of white cuffs and a collar. However, she brushed the green moss from his sleeve with some toweling, and although this operation brought her so near to him that her breath--as soft and warm as the southwest trades--stirred his hair, it was evident that this contiguity was only frontier familiarity, as far removed from conscious coquetry as it was, perhaps, from educated delicacy.

"The boys gin'rally kem to take up enough wood for me to begin with," she said, "but I reckon they didn't know I was comin' up so soon."

Hemmingway's distrust returned a little at this obvious suggestion that he was only a substitute for their general gallantry, but he smiled and said somewhat bluntly, "I don't suppose you lack for admirers here."

The girl, however, took him literally. "Lordy, no! Me and Mamie Robinson are the only girls for fifteen miles along the creek. ADMIRIN'! I call it jest PESTERIN' sometimes! I reckon I'll hev to keep a dog!"

Hemmingway shivered. Yes, she was not only conscious, but spoilt already. He pictured to himself the uncouth gallantries of the settlement, the provincial badinage, the feeble rivalries of the young men whom he had seen at the general store. Undoubtedly this was what she was expecting in HIM!

"Well," she said, turning from the fire she had kindled, "while I'm settin' the table, tell me what's a-doin' in Sacramento! I reckon you've got heaps of lady friends thar,--I'm told there's lots of fashions just from the States."

"I'm afraid I don't know enough of them to interest you," he said dryly.

"Go on and talk," she replied. "Why, when Tom Flynn kem back from Sacramento, and he warn't thar more nor a week, he jest slung yarns about his doin's thar to last the hull rainy season."

Half amused and half annoyed, Hemmingway seated himself on the little platform beside the open door, and began a conscientious description of the progress of Sacramento, its new buildings, hotels, and theatres, as it had struck him on his last visit. For a while he was somewhat entertained by the girl's vivacity and eager questioning, but presently it began to pall. He continued, however, with a grim sense of duty, and partly as a reason for watching her in her household duties. Certainly she was graceful! Her tall, lithe, but beautifully moulded figure, even in its characteristic southwestern indolence, fell into poses as picturesque as they were unconscious. She lifted the big molasses-can from its shelf on the rafters with the attitude of a Greek water-bearer. She upheaved the heavy flour-sack to the same secure shelf with the upraised palms of an Egyptian caryatid. Suddenly she interrupted Hemmingway's perfunctory talk with a hearty laugh. He started, looked up from his seat on the platform, and saw that she was standing over him and regarding him with a kind of mischievous pity.

"Look here," she said, "I reckon that'll do! You kin pull up short! I kin see what's the matter with you; you're jest plumb tired, tuckered out, and want to turn in! So jest you sit that quiet until I get supper ready and never mind me." In vain Hemmingway protested, with a rising color. The girl only shook her head. "Don't tell me! You ain't keering to talk, and you're only playin' Sacramento statistics on me," she retorted, with unfeigned cheerfulness. "Anyhow, here's the wimmen comin', and supper is ready."

There was a sound of weary, resigned ejaculations and pantings, and three gaunt women in lustreless alpaca gowns appeared before the cabin. They seemed prematurely aged and worn with labor, anxiety, and ill nourishment. Doubtless somewhere in these ruins a flower like Jay Jules had once flourished; doubtless somewhere in that graceful nymph herself the germ of this dreary maturity was hidden. Hemmingway welcomed them with a seriousness equal to their own. The supper was partaken with the kind of joyless formality which in the southwest is supposed to indicate deep respect, even the cheerful Jay falling under the influence, and it was with a feeling of relief that at last the young man retired to his fenced-off corner for solitude and repose. He gathered, however, that before "sun up" the next morning the elder women were going to Rattlesnake Bar for the weekly shopping, leaving Jay as before to prepare his breakfast and then join them later. It was already a change in his sentiments to find himself looking forward to that tete-a-tete with the young girl, as a chance of redeeming his character in her eyes. He was beginning to feel he had been stupid, unready, and withal prejudiced. He undressed himself in his seclusion, broken only by the monotonous voices in the adjoining apartment.

From time to time he heard fragments and scraps of their conversation, always in reference to affairs of the household and settlement, but never of himself,--not even the suggestion of a prudent lowering of their voices,--and fell asleep. He woke up twice in the night with a sensation of cold so marked and distinct from his experience of the early evening, that he was fain to pile his clothes over his blankets to keep warm. He fell asleep again, coming once more to consciousness with a sense of a slight jar, but relapsing again into slumber for he knew not how long. Then he was fully awakened by a voice calling him, and, opening his eyes, beheld the blanket partition put aside, and the face of Jay thrust forward. To his surprise it wore a look of excited astonishment dominated by irrepressible laughter.

"Get up quick as you kin," she said gaspingly; "this is about the killingest thing that ever happened!"

She disappeared, but he could still hear her laughing, and to his utter astonishment with her disappearance the floor seemed to change its level. A giddy feeling seized him; he put his feet to the floor; it was unmistakably wet and oozing. He hurriedly clothed himself, still accompanied by the strange feeling of oscillation and giddiness, and passed though the opening into the next room. Again his step produced the same effect upon the floor, and he actually stumbled against her shaking figure, as she wiped the tears of uncontrollable mirth from her eyes with her apron. The contact seemed to upset her remaining gravity. She dropped into a chair, and, pointing to the open door, gasped, "Look thar! Lordy! How's that for high?" threw her apron over her head, and gave way to an uproarious fit of laughter.

Hemmingway turned to the open door. A lake was before him on the level of the cabin. He stepped forward on the platform; the water was right and left, all around him. The platform dipped slightly to his step. The cabin was afloat,--afloat upon its base of logs like a raft, the whole structure upheld by the floor on which the logs were securely fastened. The high ground had disappeared--the river--its banks the green area beyond. They, and THEY alone, were afloat upon an inland sea.

He turned an astounded and serious face upon her mirth. "When did it happen?" he demanded. She checked her laugh, more from a sense of polite deference to his mood than any fear, and said quietly, "That gets me. Everything was all right two hours ago when the wimmen left. It was too early to get your breakfast and rouse ye out, and I felt asleep, I reckon, until I felt a kind o' slump and a jar." Hemmingway remembered his own half-conscious sensation. "Then I got up and saw we was adrift. I didn't waken ye, for I thought it was only a sort of wave that would pass. It wasn't until I saw we were movin' and the hull rising ground gettin' away, that I thought o' callin' ye."

He thought of the vanished general store, of her father, the workers on the bank, the helpless women on their way to the Bar, and turned almost savagely on her.

"But the others,--where are they?" he said indignantly. "Do you call that a laughing matter?"

She stopped at the sound of his voice as at a blow. Her face hardened into immobility, yet when she replied it was with the deliberate indolence of her father. "The wimmen are up on the hills by this time. The boys hev bin drowned out many times afore this and got clear off, on sluice boxes and timber, without squealing. Tom Flynn went down ten miles to Sayer's once on two bar'ls, and I never heard that HE was cryin' when they picked him up."

A flush came to Hemmingway's cheek, but with it a gleam of intelligence. Of course the inundation was known to them FIRST, and there was the wreckage to support them. They had clearly saved themselves. If they had abandoned the cabin, it was because they knew its security, perhaps had even seen it safely adrift.

"Has this ever happened to the cabin before?" he asked, as he thought of its peculiar base.

"No."

He looked at the water again. There was a decided current. The overflow was evidently no part of the original inundation. He put his hand in the water. It was icy cold. Yes, he understood it now. It was the sudden melting of snow in the Sierras which had brought this volume down the canyon. But was there more still to come?

"Have you anything like a long pole or stick in the cabin?"

"Nary," said the girl, opening her big eyes and shaking her head with a simulation of despair, which was, however, flatly contradicted by her laughing mouth.

"Nor any cord or twine?" he continued.

She handed him a ball of coarse twine.

"May I take a couple of these hooks?" he asked, pointing to some rough iron hooks in the rafters, on which bacon and jerked beef were hanging.

She nodded. He dislodged the hooks, greased them with the bacon rind, and affixed them to the twine.

"Fishin'?" she asked demurely.

"Exactly," he replied gravely.

He threw the line in the water. It slackened at about six feet, straightened, and became taut at an angle, and then dragged. After one or two sharp jerks he pulled it up. A few leaves and grasses were caught in the hooks. He examined them attentively.

"We're not in the creek," he said, "nor in the old overflow. There's no mud or gravel on the hooks, and these grasses don't grow near water."

"Now, that's mighty cute of you," she said admiringly, as she knelt beside him on the platform. "Let's see what you've caught. Look yer!" she added, suddenly lifting a limp stalk, "that's 'old man,' and thar ain't a scrap of it grows nearer than Springer's Rise,--four miles from home."

"Are you sure?" he asked quickly.

"Sure as pop! I used to go huntin' it for smellidge."

"For what?" he said, with a bewildered smile.

"For this,"--she thrust the leaves to his nose and then to her own pink nostrils; "for--for"--she hesitated, and then with a mischievous simulation of correctness added, "for the perfume."

He looked at her admiringly. For all her five feet ten inches, what a mere child she was, after all! What a fool he was to have taken a resentful attitude towards her! How charming and graceful she looked, kneeling there beside him!

"Tell me," he said suddenly, in a gentler voice, "what were you laughing at just now?"

Her brown eyes wavered for a moment, and then brimmed with merriment. She threw herself sideways, in a leaning posture, supporting herself on one arm, while with her other hand she slowly drew out her apron string, as she said, in a demure voice:--

"Well, I reckoned it was jest too killin' to think of you, who didn't want to talk to me, and would hev given your hull pile to hev skipped out o' this, jest stuck here alongside o' me, whether you would or no, for Lord knows how long!"

"But that was last night," he said, in a tone of raillery. "I was tired, and you said so yourself, you know. But I'm ready to talk now. What shall I tell you?"

"Anything," said the girl, with a laugh.

"What I am thinking of?" he said, with frankly admiring eyes.

"Yes."

"Everything?"

"Yes, everything." She stopped, and leaning forward, suddenly caught the brim of his soft felt hat, and drawing it down smartly over his audacious eyes, said, "Everything BUT THAT."

It was with some difficulty and some greater embarrassment that he succeeded in getting his eyes free again. When he did so, she had risen and entered the cabin. Disconcerted as he was, he was relieved to see that her expression of amusement was unchanged. Was her act a piece of rustic coquetry, or had she resented his advances? Nor did her next words settle the question.

"Ye kin do yer nice talk and philanderin' after we've settled whar we are, what we're goin', and what's goin' to happen. Jest now it 'pears to me that ez these yere logs are the only thing betwixt us and 'kingdom come,' ye'd better be hustlin' round with a few spikes to clinch 'em to the floor."

She handed him a hammer and a few spikes. He obediently set to work, with little confidence, however, in the security of the fastening. There was neither rope nor chain for lashing the logs together; a stronger current and a collision with some submerged stump or wreckage would loosen them and wreck the cabin. But he said nothing. It was the girl who broke the silence.

"What's your front name?"

"Miles."

"MILES,--that's a funny name. I reckon that's why you war so FAR OFF and DISTANT at first."

Mr. Hemmingway thought this very witty, and said so. "But," he added, "when I was a little nearer a moment ago, you stopped me."

"But you was moving faster than the shanty was. I reckon you don't take that gait with your lady friends at Sacramento! However, you kin talk now."

"But you forget I don't know 'where we are,' nor 'what's going to happen.'"

"But I do," she said quietly. "In a couple of hours we'll be picked up, so you'll be free again."

Something in the confidence of her manner made him go to the door again and look out. There was scarcely any current now, and the cabin seemed motionless. Even the wind, which might have acted upon it, was wanting. They were apparently in the same position as before, but his sounding-line showed that the water was slightly falling. He came back and imparted the fact with a certain confidence born of her previous praise of his knowledge. To his surprise she only laughed and said lazily, "We'll be all right, and you'll be free, in about two hours."

"I see no sign of it," he said, looking through the door again.

"That's because you're looking in the water and the sky and the mud for it," she said, with a laugh. "I reckon you've been trained to watch them things a heap better than to study the folks about here."

"I daresay you're right," said Hemmingway cheerfully, "but I don't clearly see what the folks about here have to do with our situation just now."

"You'll see," she said, with a smile of mischievous mystery. "All the same," she added, with a sudden and dangerous softness in her eyes, "I ain't sayin' that YOU ain't kinder right neither."

An hour ago he would have laughed at the thought that a mere look and sentence like this from the girl could have made his heart beat. "Then I may go on and talk?"

She smiled, but her eyes said, "Yes," plainly.

He turned to take a chair near her. Suddenly the cabin trembled, there was a sound of scraping, a bump, and then the whole structure tilted to one side and they were both thrown violently towards the corner, with a swift inrush of water. Hemmingway quickly caught the girl by the waist; she clung to him instinctively, yet still laughing, as with a desperate effort he succeeded in dragging her to the upper side of the slanting cabin, and momentarily restoring its equilibrium. They remained for an instant breathless. But in that instant he had drawn her face to his and kissed her.

She disengaged herself gently with neither excitement nor emotion, and pointing to the open door said, "Look there!"

Two of the logs which formed the foundation of their floor were quietly floating in the water before the cabin! The submerged obstacle or snag which had torn them from their fastening was still holding the cabin fast. Hemmingway saw the danger. He ran along the narrow ledge to the point of contact and unhesitatingly leaped into the icy cold water. It reached his armpits before his feet struck the obstacle,--evidently a stump with a projecting branch. Bracing himself against it, he shoved off the cabin. But when he struck out to follow it, he found that the log nearest him was loose and his grasp might tear it away. At the same moment, however, a pink calico arm fluttered above his head, and a strong grasp seized his coat collar. The cabin half revolved as the girl dragged him into the open door.

"You bantam!" she said, with a laugh, "why didn't you let ME do that? I'm taller than you! But," she added, looking at his dripping clothes and dragging out a blanket from the corner, "I couldn't dry myself as quick as you kin!" To her surprise, however, Hemmingway tossed the blanket aside, and pointing to the floor, which was already filmed with water, ran to the still warm stove, detached it from its pipe, and threw it overboard. The sack of flour, bacon, molasses, and sugar, and all the heavier articles followed it into the stream. Relieved of their weight the cabin base rose an inch or two higher. Then he sat down and said, "There! that may keep us afloat for that 'couple of hours' you speak of. So I suppose I may talk now!"

"Ye haven't no time," she said, in a graver voice. "It won't be as long as a couple of hours now. Look over thar!"

He looked where she pointed across the gray expanse of water. At first he could see nothing. Presently he saw a mere dot on its face which at times changed to a single black line.

"It's a log, like these," he said.

"It's no log. It's an Injun dug-out*--comin' for me."

   * A canoe made from a hollowed log.

"Your father?" he said joyfully.

She smiled pityingly. "It's Tom Flynn. Father's got suthin' else to look arter. Tom Flynn hasn't."

"And who's Tom Flynn?" he asked, with an odd sensation.

"The man I'm engaged to," she said gravely, with a slight color.

The rose that blossomed on her cheek faded in his. There was a moment of silence. Then he said frankly, "I owe you some apology. Forgive my folly and impertinence a moment ago. How could I have known this?"

"You took no more than you deserved, or that Tom would have objected to," she said, with a little laugh. "You've been mighty kind and handy."

She held out her hand; their fingers closed together in a frank pressure. Then his mind went back to his work, which he had forgotten,--to his first impressions of the camp and of her. They both stood silent, watching the canoe, now quite visible, and the man that was paddling it, with an intensity that both felt was insincere.

"I'm afraid," he said, with a forced laugh, "that I was a little too hasty in disposing of your goods and possessions. We could have kept afloat a little longer."

"It's all the same," she said, with a slight laugh; "it's jest as well we didn't look too comf'ble--to HIM."

He did not reply; he did not dare to look at her. Yes! It was the same coquette he had seen last night. His first impressions were correct.

The canoe came on rapidly now, propelled by a powerful arm. In a few moments it was alongside, and its owner leaped on the platform. It was the gentleman with his trousers tucked in his boots, the second voice in the gloomy discussion in the general store last evening. He nodded simply to the girl, and shook Hemmingway's hand warmly.

Then he made a hurried apology for his delay: it was so difficult to find "the lay" of the drifted cabin. He had struck out first for the most dangerous spot,--the "old clearing," on the right bank, with its stumps and new growths,--and it seemed he was right. And all the rest were safe, and "nobody was hurt."

"All the same, Tom," she said, when they were seated and paddling off again, "you don't know HOW NEAR YOU CAME TO LOSING ME." Then she raised her beautiful eyes and looked significantly, not at HIM, but at Hemmingway.

When the water was down at "Jules'" the next day, they found certain curious changes and some gold, and the secretary was able to make a favorable report. But he made none whatever of his impressions "when the water was up at 'Jules'," though he often wondered if they were strictly trustworthy.

THE BOOM IN THE "CALAVERAS CLARION"

The editorial sanctum of the "Calaveras Clarion" opened upon the "composing-room" of that paper on the one side, and gave apparently upon the rest of Calaveras County upon the other. For, situated on the very outskirts of the settlement and the summit of a very steep hill, the pines sloped away from the editorial windows to the long valley of the South Fork and--infinity. The little wooden building had invaded Nature without subduing it. It was filled night and day with the murmur of pines and their fragrance. Squirrels scampered over its roof when it was not preoccupied by woodpeckers, and a printer's devil had once seen a nest-building blue jay enter the composing window, flutter before one of the slanting type-cases with an air of deliberate selection, and then fly off with a vowel in its bill.

Amidst these sylvan surroundings the temporary editor of the "Clarion" sat at his sanctum, reading the proofs of an editorial. As he was occupying that position during a six weeks' absence of the bona fide editor and proprietor, he was consequently reading the proof with some anxiety and responsibility. It had been suggested to him by certain citizens that the "Clarion" needed a firmer and more aggressive policy towards the Bill before the Legislature for the wagon road to the South Fork. Several Assembly men had been "got at" by the rival settlement of Liberty Hill, and a scathing exposure and denunciation of such methods was necessary. The interests of their own township were also to be "whooped up." All this had been vigorously explained to him, and he had grasped the spirit, if not always the facts, of his informants. It is to be feared, therefore, that he was perusing his article more with reference to its vigor than his own convictions. And yet he was not so greatly absorbed as to be unmindful of the murmur of the pines without, his half-savage environment, and the lazy talk of his sole companions,--the foreman and printer in the adjoining room.

"Bet your life! I've always said that a man INSIDE a newspaper office could hold his own agin any outsider that wanted to play rough or tried to raid the office! Thar's the press, and thar's the printin' ink and roller! Folks talk a heap o' the power o' the Press!--I tell ye, ye don't half know it. Why, when old Kernel Fish was editin' the 'Sierra Banner,' one o' them bullies that he'd lampooned in the 'Banner' fought his way past the Kernel in the office, into the composin'-room, to wreck everythin' and 'pye' all the types. Spoffrel--ye don't remember Spoffrel?--little red-haired man?--was foreman. Spoffrel fended him off with the roller and got one good dab inter his eyes that blinded him, and then Spoffrel sorter skirmished him over to the press,--a plain lever just like ours,--whar the locked-up form of the inside was still a-lyin'! Then, quick as lightnin', Spoffrel tilts him over agin it, and HE throws out his hand and ketches hold o' the form to steady himself, when Spoffrel just runs the form and the hand under the press and down with the lever! And that held the feller fast as grim death! And when at last he begs off, and Spoff lets him loose, the hull o' that 'ere lampooning article he objected to was printed right onto the skin o' his hand! Fact, and it wouldn't come off, either."

"Gosh, but I'd like to hev seen it," said the printer. "There ain't any chance, I reckon, o' such a sight here. The boss don't take no risks lampoonin', and he" (the editor knew he was being indicated by some unseen gesture of the unseen work-man) "ain't that style."

"Ye never kin tell," said the foreman didactically, "what might happen! I've known editors to get into a fight jest for a little innercent bedevilin' o' the opposite party. Sometimes for a misprint. Old man Pritchard of the 'Argus' oncet had a hole blown through his arm because his proofreader had called Colonel Starbottle's speech an 'ignominious' defense, when the old man hed written 'ingenuous' defense."

The editor paused in his proof-reading. He had just come upon the sentence: "We cannot congratulate Liberty Hill--in its superior elevation--upon the ignominious silence of the representative of all Calaveras when this infamous Bill was introduced." He referred to his copy. Yes! He had certainly written "ignominious,"--that was what his informants had suggested. But was he sure they were right? He had a vague recollection, also, that the representative alluded to--Senator Bradley--

had fought two duels, and was a "good" though somewhat impulsive shot! He might alter the word to "ingenuous" or "ingenious," either would be finely sarcastic, but then--there was his foreman, who would detect it! He would wait until he had finished the entire article. In that occupation he became oblivious of the next room, of a silence, a whispered conversation, which ended with a rapping at the door and the appearance of the foreman in the doorway.

"There's a man in the office who wants to see the editor," he said.

"Show him in," replied the editor briefly. He was, however, conscious that there was a singular significance in his foreman's manner, and an eager apparition of the other printer over the foreman's shoulder.

"He's carryin' a shot-gun, and is a man twice as big as you be," said the foreman gravely.

The editor quickly recalled his own brief and as yet blameless record in the "Clarion." "Perhaps," he said tentatively, with a gentle smile, "he's looking for Captain Brush" (the absent editor).

"I told him all that," said the foreman grimly, "and he said he wanted to see the man in charge."

In proportion as the editor's heart sank his outward crest arose. "Show him in," he said loftily.

"We KIN keep him out," suggested the foreman, lingering a moment; "me and him," indicating the expectant printer behind him, "is enough for that."

"Show him up," repeated the editor firmly.

The foreman withdrew; the editor seated himself and again took up his proof. The doubtful word "ignominious" seemed to stand out of the paragraph before him; it certainly WAS a strong expression! He was about to run his pencil through it when he heard the heavy step of his visitor approaching. A sudden instinct of belligerency took possession of him, and he wrathfully threw the pencil down.

The burly form of the stranger blocked the doorway. He was dressed like a miner, but his build and general physiognomy were quite distinct from the local variety. His upper lip and chin were clean-shaven, still showing the blue-black roots of the beard which covered the rest of his face and depended in a thick fleece under his throat. He carried a small bundle tied up in a silk handkerchief in one hand, and a "shot-gun" in the other, perilously at half-cock. Entering the sanctum, he put down his bundle and quietly closed the door behind him. He then drew an empty chair towards him and dropped heavily into it with his gun on his knees. The editor's heart dropped almost as heavily, although he quite composedly held out his hand.

"Shall I relieve you of your gun?"

"Thank ye, lad--noa. It's moor coomfortable wi' me, and it's main dangersome to handle on the half-cock. That's why I didn't leave 'im on the horse outside!"

At the sound of his voice and occasional accent a flash of intelligence relieved the editor's mind. He remembered that twenty miles away, in the illimitable vista from his windows, lay a settlement of English north-country miners, who, while faithfully adopting the methods, customs, and even slang of the Californians, retained many of their native peculiarities. The gun he carried on his knee, however, was evidently part of the Californian imitation.

"Can I do anything for you?" said the editor blandly.

"Ay! I've coom here to bill ma woife."

"I--don't think I understand," hesitated the editor, with a smile.

"I've coom here to get ye to put into your paaper a warnin', a notiss, that onless she returns to my house in four weeks, I'll have nowt to do wi' her again."

"Oh!" said the editor, now perfectly reassured, "you want an advertisement? That's the business of the foreman; I'll call him." He was rising from his seat when the stranger laid a heavy hand on his shoulder and gently forced him down again.

"Noa, lad! I don't want noa foreman nor understrappers to take this job. I want to talk it over wi' you. Sabe? My woife she bin up and awaa these six months. We had a bit of difference, that ain't here nor there, but she skedaddled outer my house. I want to give her fair warning, and let her know I ain't payin' any debts o' hers arter this notiss, and I ain't takin' her back arter four weeks from date."

"I see," said the editor glibly. "What's your wife's name?"

"Eliza Jane Dimmidge."

"Good," continued the editor, scribbling on the paper before him; "something like this will do: 'Whereas my wife, Eliza Jane Dimmidge, having left my bed and board without just cause or provocation, this is to give notice that I shall not be responsible for any debts of her contracting on or after this date.'"

"Ye must be a lawyer," said Mr. Dimmidge admiringly.

It was an old enough form of advertisement, and the remark showed incontestably that Mr. Dimmidge was not a native; but the editor smiled patronizingly and went on: "'And I further give notice that if she does not return within the period of four weeks from this date, I shall take such proceedings for relief as the law affords.'"

"Coom, lad, I didn't say THAT."

"But you said you wouldn't take her back."

"Ay."

"And you can't prevent her without legal proceedings. She's your wife. But you needn't take proceedings, you know. It's only a warning."

Mr. Dimmidge nodded approvingly. "That's so."

"You'll want it published for four weeks, until date?" asked the editor.

"Mebbe longer, lad."

The editor wrote "till forbid" in the margin of the paper and smiled.

"How big will it be?" said Mr. Dimmidge.

The editor took up a copy of the "Clarion" and indicated about an inch of space. Mr. Dimmidge's face fell.

"I want it bigger,--in large letters, like a play-card," he said. "That's no good for a warning."

"You can have half a column or a whole column if you like," said the editor airily.

"I'll take a whole one," said Mr. Dimmidge simply.

The editor laughed. "Why! it would cost you a hundred dollars."

"I'll take it," repeated Mr. Dimmidge.

"But," said the editor gravely, "the same notice in a small space will serve your purpose and be quite legal."

"Never you mind that, lad! It's the looks of the thing I'm arter, and not the expense. I'll take that column."

The editor called in the foreman and showed him the copy. "Can you display that so as to fill a column?"

The foreman grasped the situation promptly. It would be big business for the paper. "Yes," he said meditatively, "that bold-faced election type will do it."

Mr. Dimmidge's face brightened. The expression "bold-faced" pleased him.

"That's it! I told you. I want to bill her in a portion of the paper."

"I might put in a cut," said the foreman suggestively; "something like this." He took a venerable woodcut from the case. I grieve to say it was one which, until the middle of the present century, was common enough in the newspaper offices in the Southwest. It showed the running figure of a negro woman carrying her personal property in a knotted handkerchief slung from a stick over her shoulder, and was supposed to represent "a fugitive slave."

Mr. Dimmidge's eyes brightened. "I'll take that, too. It's a little dark-complected for Mrs. P., but it will do. Now roon away, lad," he said to the foreman, as he quietly pushed him into the outer office again and closed the door. Then, facing the surprised editor, he said, "Theer's another notiss I want ye to put in your paper; but that's atween US. Not a word to THEM," he indicated the banished foreman with a jerk of his thumb. "Sabe? I want you to put this in another part o' your paper, quite innocent-like, ye know." He drew from his pocket a gray wallet, and taking out a slip of paper read from it gravely, "'If this should meet the eye of R. B., look out for M. J. D. He is on your track. When this you see write a line to E. J. D., Elktown Post Office.' I want this to go in as 'Personal and Private'--sabe?--like them notisses in the big 'Frisco papers."

"I see," said the editor, laying it aside. "It shall go in the same issue in another column."

Apparently Mr. Dimmidge expected something more than this reply, for after a moment's hesitation he said with an odd smile:

"Ye ain't seein' the meanin' o' that, lad?"

"No," said the editor lightly; "but I suppose R. B. does, and it isn't intended that any one else should."

"Mebbe it is, and mebbe it isn't," said Mr. Dimmidge, with a self-satisfied air. "I don't mind saying atween us that R. B. is the man as I've suspicioned as havin' something to do with my wife goin' away; and ye see, if he writes to E. J. D.--that's my wife's initials--at Elktown, I'LL get that letter and so make sure."

"But suppose your wife goes there first, or sends?"

"Then I'll ketch her or her messenger. Ye see?"

The editor did not see fit to oppose any argument to this phenomenal simplicity, and Mr. Dimmidge, after settling his bill with the foreman, and enjoining the editor to the strictest secrecy regarding the origin of the "personal notice," took up his gun and departed, leaving the treasury of the "Clarion" unprecedentedly enriched, and the editor to his proofs.

The paper duly appeared the next morning with the column advertisement, the personal notice, and the weighty editorial on the wagon road. There was a singular demand for the paper, the edition was speedily exhausted, and the editor was proportionately flattered, although he was surprised to receive neither praise nor criticism from his subscribers. Before evening, however, he learned to his astonishment that the excitement was caused by the column advertisement. Nobody knew Mr. Dimmidge, nor his domestic infelicities, and the editor and foreman, being equally in the dark, took refuge in a mysterious and impressive evasion of all inquiry. Never since the last San Francisco Vigilance Committee had the office been so besieged. The editor, foreman, and even the apprentice, were buttonholed and "treated" at the bar, but to no effect. All that could be learned was that it was a bona fide advertisement, for which one hundred dollars had been received! There were great discussions and conflicting theories as to whether the value of the wife, or the husband's anxiety to get rid of her, justified the enormous expense and ostentatious display. She was supposed to be an exceedingly beautiful woman by some, by others a perfect Sycorax; in one breath Mr. Dimmidge was a weak, uxorious spouse, wasting his substance on a creature who did not care for him, and in another a maddened, distracted, henpecked man, content to purchase peace and rest at any price. Certainly, never was advertisement more effective in its publicity, or cheaper in proportion to the circulation it commanded. It was copied throughout the whole Pacific slope; mighty San Francisco papers described its size and setting under the attractive headline, "How they Advertise a Wife in the Mountains!" It reappeared in the Eastern journals, under the title of "Whimsicalities of the Western Press." It was believed to have crossed to England as a specimen of "Transatlantic Savagery." The real editor of the "Clarion" awoke one morning, in San Francisco, to find his paper famous. Its advertising columns were eagerly sought for; he at once advanced the rates. People bought successive issues to gaze upon this monumental record of extravagance. A singular idea, which, however, brought further fortune to the paper, was advanced by an astute critic at the Eureka Saloon. "My opinion, gentlemen, is that the whole blamed thing is a bluff! There ain't no Mr. Dimmidge; there ain't no Mrs. Dimmidge; there ain't no desertion! The whole rotten thing is an ADVER-TISEMENT o' suthin'! Ye'll find afore ye get through with it that that there wife won't come back until that blamed husband buys Somebody's Soap, or treats her to Somebody's particular Starch or Patent Medicine! Ye jest watch and see!" The idea was startling, and seized upon the mercantile mind. The principal merchant of the town, and purveyor to the mining settlements beyond, appeared the next morning at the office of the "Clarion." "Ye wouldn't mind puttin' this 'ad' in a column along-side o' the Dimmidge one, would ye?" The young editor glanced at it, and then, with a serpent-like sagacity, veiled, however, by the suavity of the dove, pointed out that the original advertiser might think it called his bona fides into question and withdraw his advertisement. "But if we secured you by an offer of double the amount per column?" urged the merchant. "That," responded the locum tenens, "was for the actual editor and proprietor in San Francisco to determine. He would telegraph." He did so. The response was, "Put it in." Whereupon in the next issue, side by side with Mr. Dimmidge's protracted warning, appeared a column with the announcement, in large letters, "WE HAVEN'T LOST ANY WIFE, but WE are prepared to furnish the following goods at a lower rate than any other advertiser in the county," followed by the usual price list of the merchant's wares. There was an unprecedented demand for that issue. The reputation of the "Clarion," both as a shrewd advertising medium and a comic paper, was established at once. For a few days the editor waited with some apprehension for a remonstrance from the absent Dimmidge, but none came. Whether Mr. Dimmidge recognized that this new ad-vertisement gave extra publicity to his own, or that he was already on the track of the fugitive, the editor did not know. The few curious citizens who had, early in the excitement, penetrated the settlement of the English miners twenty miles away in search of information, found that Mr. Dimmidge had gone away, and that Mrs. Dimmidge had NEVER resided there with him!

Six weeks passed. The limit of Mr. Dimmidge's advertisement had been reached, and, as it was not renewed, it had passed out of the pages of the "Clarion," and with it the merchant's advertisement in the next column. The excitement had subsided, although its influence was still felt in the circulation of the paper and its advertising popularity. The temporary editor was also nearing the limit of his incumbency, but had so far participated in the good fortune of the "Clarion" as to receive an offer from one of the San Francisco dailies.

It was a warm night, and he was alone in his sanctum. The rest of the building was dark and deserted, and his solitary light, flashing out through the open window, fell upon the nearer pines and was lost in the dark, indefinable slope below. He had reached the sanctum by the rear, and a door which he also left open to enjoy the freshness of the aromatic air. Nor did it in the least mar his privacy. Rather the solitude of the great woods without seemed to enter through that door and encompassed him with its protecting loneliness. There was occasionally a faint "peep" in the scant eaves, or a "pat-pat," ending in a frightened scurry across the roof, or the slow flap of a heavy wing in the darkness below. These gentle disturbances did not, however, interrupt his work on "The True Functions of the County Newspaper," the editorial on which he was engaged.

Presently a more distinct rustling against the straggling blackberry bushes beside the door attracted his attention. It was followed by a light tapping against the side of the house. The editor started and turned quickly towards the open door. Two outside steps led to the ground. Standing upon the lower one was a woman. The upper part of her figure, illuminated by the light from the door, was thrown into greater relief by the dark background of the pines. Her face was unknown to him, but it was a pleasant one, marked by a certain good-humored determination.

"May I come in?" she said confidently.

"Certainly," said the editor. "I am working here alone because it is so quiet." He thought he would precipitate some explanation from her by excusing himself.

"That's the reason why I came," she said, with a quiet smile.

She came up the next step and entered the room. She was plainly but neatly dressed, and now that her figure was revealed he saw that she was wearing a linsey-woolsey riding-skirt, and carried a serviceable rawhide whip in her cotton-gauntleted hand. She took the chair he offered her and sat down sideways on it, her whip hand now also holding up her skirt, and permitting a hem of clean white petticoat and a smart, well-shaped boot to be seen.

"I don't remember to have had the pleasure of seeing you in Calaveras before," said the editor tentatively.

"No. I never was here before," she said composedly, "but you've heard enough of me, I reckon. I'm Mrs. Dimmidge." She threw one hand over the back of the chair, and with the other tapped her riding-whip on the floor.

The editor started. Mrs. Dimmidge! Then she was not a myth. An absurd similarity between her attitude with the whip and her husband's entrance with his gun six weeks before forced itself upon him and made her an invincible presence.

"Then you have returned to your husband?" he said hesitatingly.

"Not much!" she returned, with a slight curl of her lip.

"But you read his advertisement?"

"I saw that column of fool nonsense he put in your paper--ef that's what you mean," she said with decision, "but I didn't come here to see HIM--but YOU."

The editor looked at her with a forced smile, but a vague misgiving. He was alone at night in a deserted part of the settlement, with a plump, self-possessed woman who had a contralto voice, a horsewhip, and--he could not help feeling--an evident grievance.

"To see me?" he repeated, with a faint attempt at gallantry. "You are paying me a great compliment, but really"--

"When I tell you I've come three thousand miles from Kansas straight here without stopping, ye kin reckon it's so," she replied firmly.

"Three thousand miles!" echoed the editor wonderingly.

"Yes. Three thousand miles from my own folks' home in Kansas, where six years ago I married Mr. Dimmidge,--a British furriner as could scarcely make himself understood in any Christian language! Well, he got round me and dad, allowin' he was a reg'lar out-and-out profeshnal miner,--had lived in mines ever since he was a boy; and so, not knowin' what kind o' mines, and dad just bilin' over with the gold fever, we were married and kem across the plains to Californy. He was a good enough man to look at, but it warn't three months before I discovered that he allowed a wife was no better nor a nigger slave, and he the master. That made me open my eyes; but then, as he didn't drink, and didn't gamble, and didn't swear, and was a good provider and laid by money, why I shifted along with him as best I could. We drifted down the first year to Sonora, at Red Dog, where there wasn't another woman. Well, I did the nigger slave business,--never stirring out o' the settlement, never seein' a town or a crowd o' decent people,--and he did the lord and master! We played that game for two years, and I got tired. But when at last he allowed he'd go up to Elktown Hill, where there was a passel o' his countrymen at work, with never a sign o' any other folks, and leave me alone at Red Dog until he fixed up a place for me at Elktown Hill,--I kicked! I gave him fair warning! I did as other nigger slaves did,--I ran away!"

A recollection of the wretched woodcut which Mr. Dimmidge had selected to personify his wife flashed upon the editor with a new meaning. Yet perhaps she had not seen it, and had only read a copy of the advertisement. What could she want? The "Calaveras Clarion," although a "Palladium" and a "Sentinel upon the Heights of Freedom" in reference to wagon roads, was not a redresser of domestic wrongs,--except through its advertising columns! Her next words intensified that suggestion.

"I've come here to put an advertisement in your paper."

The editor heaved a sigh of relief, as once before. "Certainly," he said briskly. "But that's another department of the paper, and the printers have gone home. Come to-morrow morning early."

"To-morrow morning I shall be miles away," she said decisively, "and what I want done has got to be done NOW! I don't want to see no printers; I don't want ANYBODY to know I've been here but you. That's why I kem here at night, and rode all the way from Sawyer's Station, and wouldn't take the stage-coach. And when we've settled about the advertisement, I'm going to mount my horse, out thar in the bushes, and scoot outer the settlement."

"Very good," said the editor resignedly. "Of course I can deliver your instructions to the foreman. And now--let me see--I suppose you wish to intimate in a personal notice to your husband that you've returned."

"Nothin' o' the kind!" said Mrs. Dimmidge coolly. "I want to placard him as he did me. I've got it all written out here. Sabe?"

She took from her pocket a folded paper, and spreading it out on the editor's desk, with a certain pride of authorship read as follows:--

"Whereas my husband, Micah J. Dimmidge, having given out that I have left his bed and board,--the same being a bunk in a log cabin and pork and molasses three times a day,--and having advertised that he'd pay no debts of MY contractin',--which, as thar ain't any, might be easier collected than debts of his own contractin',--this is to certify that unless he returns from Elktown Hill to his only home in Sonora in one week from date, payin' the cost of this advertisement, I'll know the reason why.--Eliza Jane Dimmidge."

"Thar," she added, drawing a long breath, "put that in a column of the 'Clarion,' same size as the last, and let it work, and that's all I want of you."

"A column?" repeated the editor. "Do you know the cost is very expensive, and I COULD put it in a single paragraph?"

"I reckon I kin pay the same as Mr. Dimmidge did for HIS," said the lady complacently. "I didn't see your paper myself, but the paper as copied it--one of them big New York dailies--said that it took up a whole column."

The editor breathed more freely; she had not seen the infamous woodcut which her husband had selected. At the same moment he was struck with a sense of retribution, justice, and compensation.

"Would you," he asked hesitatingly,--"would you like it illustrated--by a cut?"

"With which?"

"Wait a moment; I'll show you."

He went into the dark composing-room, lit a candle, and rummaging in a drawer sacred to weather-beaten, old-fashioned electrotyped advertising symbols of various trades, finally selected one and brought it to Mrs. Dimmidge. It represented a bare and exceedingly stalwart arm wielding a large hammer.

"Your husband being a miner,--a quartz miner,--would that do?" he asked. (It had been previously used to advertise a blacksmith, a gold-beater, and a stonemason.)

The lady examined it critically.

"It does look a little like Micah's arm," she said meditatively. "Well--you kin put it in."

The editor was so well pleased with his success that he must needs make another suggestion. "I suppose," he said ingenuously, "that you don't want to answer the 'Personal'?"

"'Personal'?" she repeated quickly, "what's that? I ain't seen no 'Personal.'" The editor saw his blunder. She, of course, had never seen Mr. Dimmidge's artful "Personal;" THAT the big dailies naturally had not noticed nor copied. But it was too late to withdraw now. He brought out a file of the "Clarion," and snipping out the paragraph with his scissors, laid it before the lady.

She stared at it with wrinkled brows and a darkening face.

"And THIS was in the same paper?--put in by Mr. Dimmidge?" she asked breathlessly.

The editor, somewhat alarmed, stammered "Yes." But the next moment he was reassured. The wrinkles disappeared, a dozen dimples broke out where they had been, and the determined, matter-of-fact Mrs. Dimmidge burst into a fit of rosy merriment. Again and again she laughed, shaking the building, startling the sedate, melancholy woods beyond, until the editor himself laughed in sheer vacant sympathy.

"Lordy!" she said at last, gasping, and wiping the laughter from her wet eyes. "I never thought of THAT."

"No," explained the editor smilingly; "of course you didn't. Don't you see, the papers that copied the big advertisement never saw that little paragraph, or if they did, they never connected the two together."

"Oh, it ain't that," said Mrs. Dimmidge, trying to regain her composure and holding her sides. "It's that blessed DEAR old dunderhead of a Dimmidge I'm thinking of. That gets me. I see it all now. Only, sakes alive! I never thought THAT of him. Oh, it's just too much!" and she again relapsed behind her handkerchief.

"Then I suppose you don't want to reply to it," said the editor.

Her laughter instantly ceased. "Don't I?" she said, wiping her face into its previous complacent determination. "Well, young man, I reckon that's just what I WANT to do! Now, wait a moment; let's see what he said," she went on, taking up and reperusing the "Personal" paragraph. "Well, then," she went on, after a moment's silent composition with moving lips, "you just put these lines in."

The editor took up his pencil.

"To Mr. J. D. Dimmidge.--Hope you're still on R. B.'s tracks. Keep there! E. J. D."

The editor wrote down the line, and then, remembering Mr. Dimmidge's voluntary explanation of HIS "Personal," waited with some confidence for a like frankness from Mrs. Dimmidge. But he was mistaken.

"You think that he--R. B.--or Mr. Dimmidge--will understand this?" he at last asked tentatively. "Is it enough?"

"Quite enough," said Mrs. Dimmidge emphatically. She took a roll of greenbacks from her pocket, selected a hundred-dollar bill and then a five, and laid them before the editor. "Young man," she said, with a certain demure gravity, "you've done me a heap o' good. I never spent money with more satisfaction than this. I never thought much o' the 'power o' the Press,' as you call it, afore. But this has been a right comfortable visit, and I'm glad I ketched you alone. But you understand one thing: this yer visit, and WHO I am, is betwixt you and me only."

"Of course I must say that the advertisement was AUTHORIZED," returned the editor. "I'm only the temporary editor. The proprietor is away."

"So much the better," said the lady complacently. "You just say you found it on your desk with the money; but don't you give me away."

"I can promise you that the secret of your personal visit is safe with me," said the young man, with a bow, as Mrs. Dimmidge rose. "Let me see you to your horse," he added. "It's quite dark in the woods."

"I can see well enough alone, and it's just as well you shouldn't know HOW I kem or HOW I went away. Enough for you to know that I'll be miles away before that paper comes out. So stay where you are."

She pressed his hand frankly and firmly, gathered up her riding-skirt, slipped backwards to the door, and the next moment rustled away into the darkness.

Early the next morning the editor handed Mrs. Dimmidge's advertisement, and the woodcut he had selected, to his foreman. He was purposely brief in his directions, so as to avoid inquiry, and retired to his sanctum. In the space of a few moments the foreman entered with a slight embarrassment of manner.

"You'll excuse my speaking to you, sir," he said, with a singular mixture of humility and cunning. "It's no business of mine, I know; but I thought I ought to tell you that this yer kind o' thing won't pay any more,--it's about played out!"

"I don't think I understand you," said the editor loftily, but with an inward misgiving. "You don't mean to say that a regular, actual advertisement"--

"Of course, I know all that," said the foreman, with a peculiar smile; "and I'm ready to back you up in it, and so's the boy; but it won't pay."

"It HAS paid a hundred and five dollars," said the editor, taking the notes from his pocket; "so I'd advise you to simply attend to your duty and set it up."

A look of surprise, followed, however, by a kind of pitying smile, passed over the foreman's face. "Of course, sir, THAT'S all right, and you know your own business; but if you think that the new advertisement will pay this time as the other one did, and whoop up another column from an advertiser, I'm afraid you'll slip up. It's a little 'off color' now,--not 'up to date,'--if it ain't a regular 'back number,' as you'll see."

"Meantime I'll dispense with your advice," said the editor curtly, "and I think you had better let our subscribers and advertisers do the same, or the 'Clarion' might also be obliged to dispense with your SERVICES."

"I ain't no blab," said the foreman, in an aggrieved manner, "and I don't intend to give the show away even if it don't PAY. But I thought I'd tell you, because I know the folks round here better than you do."

He was right. No sooner had the advertisement appeared than the editor found that everybody believed it to be a sheer invention of his own to "once more boom" the "Clarion." If they had doubted MR. Dimmidge, they utterly rejected MRS. Dimmidge as an advertiser! It was a stale joke that nobody would follow up; and on the heels of this came a letter from the editor-in-chief.

MY DEAR BOY,--You meant well, I know, but the second Dimmidge "ad" was a mistake. Still, it was a big bluff of yours to show the money, and I send you back your hundred dollars, hoping you won't "do it again." Of course you'll have to keep the advertisement in the paper for two issues, just as if it were a real thing, and it's lucky that there's just now no pressure in our columns. You might have told a better story than that hogwash about your finding the "ad" and a hundred dollars lying loose on your desk one morning. It was rather thin, and I don't wonder the foreman kicked.

The young editor was in despair. At first he thought of writing to Mrs. Dimmidge at the Elktown Post-Office, asking her to relieve him of his vow of secrecy; but his pride forbade. There was a humorous concern, not without a touch of pity, in the faces of his contributors as he passed; a few affected to believe in the new advertisement, and asked him vague, perfunctory questions about it. His position was trying, and he was not sorry when the term of his engagement expired the next week, and he left Calaveras to take his new position on the San Francisco paper.

He was standing in the saloon of the Sacramento boat when he felt a sudden heavy pressure on his shoulder, and looking round sharply, beheld not only the black-bearded face of Mr. Dimmidge, lit up by a smile, but beside it the beaming, buxom face of Mrs. Dimmidge, overflowing with good-humor. Still a little sore from his past experience, he was about to address them abruptly, when he was utterly vanquished by the hearty pressure of their hands and the unmistakable look of gratitude in their eyes.

"I was just saying to 'Lizy Jane," began Mr. Dimmidge breathlessly, "if I could only meet that young man o' the 'Clarion' what brought us together again"--

"You'd be willin' to pay four times the amount we both paid him," interpolated the laughing Mrs. Dimmidge.

"But I didn't bring you together," burst out the dazed young man, "and I'd like to know, in the name of Heaven, what brought you together now?"

"Don't you see, lad," said the imperturbable Mr. Dimmidge, "'Lizy Jane and myself had qua'lled, and we just unpacked our fool nonsense in your paper and let the hull world know it! And we both felt kinder skeert and shamed like, and it looked such small hogwash, and of so little account, for all the talk it made, that we kinder felt lonely as two separated fools that really ought to share their foolishness together."

"And that ain't all," said Mrs. Dimmidge, with a sly glance at her spouse, "for I found out from that 'Personal' you showed me that this particular old fool was actooally jealous!--JEALOUS!"

"And then?" said the editor impatiently.

"And then I KNEW he loved me all the time."

THE SECRET OF SOBRIENTE'S WELL

Even to the eye of the most inexperienced traveler there was no doubt that Buena Vista was a "played-out" mining camp. There, seamed and scarred by hydraulic engines, was the old hillside, over whose denuded surface the grass had begun to spring again in fitful patches; there were the abandoned heaps of tailings already blackened by sun and rain, and worn into mounds like ruins of masonry; there were the waterless ditches, like giant graves, and the pools of slumgullion, now dried into shining, glazed cement. There were two or three wooden "stores," from which the windows and doors had been taken and conveyed to the newer settlement of Wynyard's Gulch. Four or five buildings that still were inhabited--the blacksmith's shop, the post-office, a pioneer's cabin, and the old hotel and stage-office--only accented the general desolation. The latter building had a remoteness of prosperity far beyond the others, having been a wayside Spanish-American posada, with adobe walls of two feet in thickness, that shamed the later shells of half-inch plank, which were slowly warping and cracking like dried pods in the oven-like heat.

The proprietor of this building, Colonel Swinger, had been looked upon by the community as a person quite as remote, old-fashioned, and inconsistent with present progress as the house itself. He was an old Virginian, who had emigrated from his decaying plantation on the James River only to find the slaves, which he had brought with him, freed men when they touched Californian soil; to be driven by Northern progress and "smartness" out of the larger cities into the mountains, to fix himself at last, with the hopeless fatuity of his race, upon an already impoverished settlement; to sink his scant capital in hopeless shafts and ledges, and finally to take over the decaying hostelry of Buena Vista, with its desultory custom and few, lingering, impecunious guests. Here, too, his old Virginian ideas of hospitality were against his financial success; he could not dun nor turn from his door those unfortunate prospectors whom the ebbing fortunes of Buena Vista had left stranded by his side.

Colonel Swinger was sitting in a wicker-work rocking-chair on the veranda of his hotel--sipping a mint julep which he held in his hand, while he gazed into the dusty distance. Nothing could have convinced him that he was not performing a serious part of his duty as hotel-keeper in this attitude, even though there were no travelers expected, and the road at this hour of the day was deserted. On a bench at his side Larry Hawkins stretched his lazy length,--one foot dropped on the veranda, and one arm occasionally groping under the bench for his own tumbler of refreshment. Apart from this community of occupation, there was apparently no interchange of sentiment between the pair. The silence had continued for some moments, when the colonel put down his glass and gazed earnestly into the distance.

"Seein' anything?" remarked the man on the bench, who had sleepily regarded him.

"No," said the colonel, "that is--it's only Dick Ruggles crossin' the road."

"Thought you looked a little startled, ez if you'd seen that ar wanderin' stranger."

"When I see that wandering stranger, sah," said the colonel decisively, "I won't be sittin' long in this yer chyar. I'll let him know in about ten seconds that I don't harbor any vagrants prowlin' about like poor whites or free niggers on my propahty, sah!"

"All the same, I kinder wish ye did see him, for you'd be settled in YOUR mind and I'd be easier in MINE, ef you found out what he was doin' round yer, or ye had to admit that it wasn't no LIVIN' man."

"What do you mean?" said the colonel, testily facing around in his chair.

His companion also altered his attitude by dropping his other foot to the floor, sitting up, and leaning lazily forward with his hands clasped.

"Look yer, colonel. When you took this place, I felt I didn't have no call to tell ye all I know about it, nor to pizen yer mind by any darned fool yarns I mout hev heard. Ye know it was one o' them old Spanish haciendas?"

"I know," said the colonel loftily, "that it was held by a grant from Charles the Fifth of Spain, just as my propahty on the James River was given to my people by

King James of England, sah!"

"That ez as may be," returned his companion, in lazy indifference; "though I reckon that Charles the Fifth of Spain and King James of England ain't got much to do with what I'm goin' to tell ye. Ye see, I was here long afore YOUR time, or any of the boys that hev now cleared out; and at that time the hacienda belonged to a man named Juan Sobriente. He was that kind o' fool that he took no stock in mining. When the boys were whoopin' up the place and finding the color everywhere, and there was a hundred men working down there in the gulch, he was either ridin' round lookin' up the wild horses he owned, or sittin' with two or three lazy peons and Injins that was fed and looked arter by the priests. Gosh! now I think of it, it was mighty like YOU when you first kem here with your niggers. That's curious, too, ain't it?"

He had stopped, gazing with an odd, superstitious wonderment at the colonel, as if overcome by this not very remarkable coincidence. The colonel, overlooking or totally oblivious to its somewhat uncomplimentary significance, simply said, "Go on. What about him?"

"Well, ez I was sayin', he warn't in it nohow, but kept on his reg'lar way when the boom was the biggest. Some of the boys allowed it was mighty oncivil for him to stand off like that, and others--when he refused a big pile for his hacienda and the garden, that ran right into the gold-bearing ledge--war for lynching him and driving him outer the settlement. But as he had a pretty darter or niece livin' with him, and, except for his partickler cussedness towards mining, was kinder peaceable and perlite, they thought better of it. Things went along like this, until one day the boys noticed--particklerly the boys that had slipped up on their luck--that old man Sobriente was gettin' rich,--had stocked a ranch over on the Divide, and had given some gold candlesticks to the mission church. That would have been only human nature and business, ef he'd had any during them flush times; but he hadn't. This kinder puzzled them. They tackled the peons,--his niggers,--but it was all 'No sabe.' They tackled another man,--a kind of half-breed Kanaka, who, except the priest, was the only man who came to see him, and was supposed to be mighty sweet on the darter or niece,--but they didn't even get the color outer HIM. Then the first thing we knowed was that old Sobriente was found dead in the well!"

"In the well, sah!" said the colonel, starting up. "The well on my propahty?"

"No," said his companion. "The old well that was afterwards shut up. Yours was dug by the last tenant, Jack Raintree, who allowed that he didn't want to 'take any Sobriente in his reg'lar whiskey and water.' Well, the half-breed Kanaka cleared out after the old man's death, and so did that darter or niece; and the church, to whom old Sobriente had left this house, let it to Raintree for next to nothin'."

"I don't see what all that has got to do with that wandering tramp," said the colonel, who was by no means pleased with this history of his property.

"I'll tell ye. A few days after Raintree took it over, he was lookin' round the garden, which old Sobriente had always kept shut up agin strangers, and he finds a lot of dried-up 'slumgullion'* scattered all about the borders and beds, just as if the old man had been using it for fertilizing. Well, Raintree ain't no fool; he allowed the old man wasn't one, either; and he knew that slumgullion wasn't worth no more than mud for any good it would do the garden. So he put this yer together with Sobriente's good luck, and allowed to himself that the old coyote had been secretly gold-washin' all the while he seemed to be standin' off agin it! But where was the mine? Whar did he get the gold? That's what got Raintree. He hunted all over the garden, prospected every part of it,--ye kin see the holes yet,--but he never even got the color!"

* That is, a viscid cement-like refuse of gold-washing.

He paused, and then, as the colonel made an impatient gesture, he went on.

"Well, one night just afore you took the place, and when Raintree was gettin' just sick of it, he happened to be walkin' in the garden. He was puzzlin' his brain agin to know how old Sobriente made his pile, when all of a suddenst he saw suthin' a-movin' in the brush beside the house. He calls out, thinkin' it was one of the boys, but got no answer. Then he goes to the bushes, and a tall figger, all in black, starts out afore him. He couldn't see any face, for its head was covered with a hood, but he saw that it held suthin' like a big cross clasped agin its breast. This made him think it was one them priests, until he looks agin and sees that it wasn't no cross it was carryin,' but a PICKAXE! He makes a jump towards it, but it vanished! He traipsed over the hull garden,--went though ev'ry bush,--but it was clean gone. Then the hull thing flashed upon him with a cold shiver. The old man bein' found dead in the well! the goin' away of the half-breed and the girl! the findin' o' that slumgullion! The old man HAD made a strike in that garden, the half-breed had discovered his secret and murdered him, throwin' him down the well! It war no LIVIN' man that he had seen, but the ghost of old Sobriente!"

The colonel emptied the remaining contents of his glass at a single gulp, and sat up. "It's my opinion, sah, that Raintree had that night more than his usual allowance of corn-juice on board; and it's only a wonder, sah, that he didn't see a few pink alligators and sky-blue snakes at the same time. But what's this got to do with that wanderin' tramp?"

"They're all the same thing, colonel, and in my opinion that there tramp ain't no more alive than that figger was."

"But YOU were the one that saw this tramp with your own eyes," retorted the colonel quickly, "and you never before allowed it was a spirit!"

"Exactly! I saw it whar a minit afore nothin' had been standin', and a minit after nothin' stood," said Larry Hawkins, with a certain serious emphasis; "but I warn't goin' to say it to ANYBODY, and I warn't goin' to give you and the hacienda away. And ez nobody knew Raintree's story, I jest shut up my head. But you kin bet your life that the man I saw warn't no livin' man!"

"We'll see, sah!" said the colonel, rising from his chair with his fingers in the armholes of his nankeen waistcoat, "ef he ever intrudes on my property again. But look yar! don't ye go sayin' anything of this to Polly,--you know what women are!"

A faint color came into Larry's face; an animation quite different to the lazy deliberation of his previous monologue shone in his eyes, as he said, with a certain rough respect he had not shown before to his companion, "That's why I'm tellin' ye, so that ef SHE happened to see anything and got skeert, ye'd know how to reason her out of it."

"'Sh!" said the colonel, with a warning gesture.

A young girl had just appeared in the doorway, and now stood leaning against the central pillar that supported it, with one hand above her head, in a lazy attitude strongly suggestive of the colonel's Southern indolence, yet with a grace entirely her own. Indeed, it overcame the negligence of her creased and faded yellow cotton frock and unbuttoned collar, and suggested--at least to the eyes of ONE man--the curving and clinging of the jasmine vine against the outer column of the veranda. Larry Hawkins rose awkwardly to his feet.

"Now what are you two men mumblin' and confidin' to each other? You look for all the world like two old women gossips," she said, with languid impertinence.

It was easy to see that a privileged and recognized autocrat spoke. No one had ever questioned Polly Swinger's right to interrupting, interfering, and saucy criticisms. Secure in the hopeless or chivalrous admiration of the men around her, she had repaid it with a frankness that scorned any coquetry; with an indifference to the ordinary feminine effect or provocation in dress or bearing that was as natural as it was invincible. No one had ever known Polly to "fix up" for anybody, yet no one ever doubted the effect, if she had. No one had ever rebuked her charming petulance, or wished to.

Larry gave a weak, vague laugh. Colonel Swinger as ineffectively assumed a mock parental severity. "When you see two gentlemen, miss, discussin' politics together, it ain't behavin' like a lady to interrupt. Better run away and tidy yourself before the stage comes."

The young lady replied to the last innuendo by taking two spirals of soft hair, like "corn silk," from her oval cheek, wetting them with her lips, and tucking them behind her ears. Her father's ungentlemanly suggestion being thus disposed of, she returned to her first charge.

"It ain't no politics; you ain't been swearing enough for THAT! Come, now! It's the mysterious stranger ye've been talking about!"

Both men stared at her with unaffected concern.

"What do YOU know about any mysterious stranger?" demanded her father.

"Do you suppose you men kin keep a secret," scoffed Polly. "Why, Dick Ruggles told me how skeert ye all were over an entire stranger, and he advised me not to wander down the road after dark. I asked him if he thought I was a pickaninny to be frightened by bogies, and that if he hadn't a better excuse for wantin' 'to see me home' from the Injin spring, he might slide."

Larry laughed again, albeit a little bitterly, for it seemed to him that the excuse was fully justified; but the colonel said promptly, "Dick's a fool, and you might have told him there were worse things to be met on the road than bogies. Run away now, and see that the niggers are on hand when the stage comes."

Two hours later the stage came with a clatter of hoofs and a cloud of red dust, which precipitated itself and a dozen thirsty travelers upon the veranda before the hotel bar-room; it brought also the usual "express" newspapers and much talk to Colonel Swinger, who always received his guests in a lofty personal fashion at the door, as he might have done in his old Virginian home; but it brought likewise--marvelous to relate--an ACTUAL GUEST, who had two trunks and asked for a room! He was evidently a stranger to the ways of Buena Vista, and particularly to those of Colonel Swinger, and at first seemed inclined to resent the social attitude of his host, and his frank and free curiosity. When he, however, found that Colonel Swinger was even better satisfied to give an account of HIS OWN affairs, his family, pedigree, and his present residence, he began to betray some interest. The colonel told him all the news, and would no doubt have even expatiated on his ghostly visitant, had he not prudently concluded that his guest might decline to remain in a haunted inn. The stranger had spoken of staying a week; he had some private mining speculations to watch at Wynyard's Gulch,--the next settlement, but he did not care to appear openly at the "Gulch Hotel." He was a man of thirty, with soft, pleasing features and a singular litheness of movement, which, combined with a nut-brown, gypsy complexion, at first suggested a foreigner. But his dialect, to the colonel's ears, was distinctly that of New England, and to this was added a puritanical and sanctimonious drawl. "He looked," said the colonel in after years, "like a blank light mulatter, but talked like a blank Yankee parson." For all that, he was acceptable to his host, who may have felt that his reminiscences of his plantation on the James River were palling on Buena Vista ears, and was glad of his new auditor. It was an advertisement, too, of the hotel, and a promise of its future fortunes. "Gentlemen having propahty interests at the Gulch, sah, prefer to stay at Buena Vista with another man of propahty, than to trust to those new-fangled papah-collared, gingerbread booths for traders that they call 'hotels' there," he had remarked to some of "the boys." In his preoccupation with the new guest, he also became a little neglectful of his old chum and dependent, Larry Hawkins. Nor was this the only circumstance that filled the head of that shiftless loyal retainer of the colonel with bitterness and foreboding. Polly Swinger--the scornfully indifferent, the contemptuously inaccessible, the coldly capricious and petulant--was inclined to be polite to the stranger!

The fact was that Polly, after the fashion of her sex, took it into her pretty head, against all consistency and logic, suddenly to make an exception to her general attitude towards mankind in favor of one individual. The reason-seeking masculine reader will rashly conclude that this individual was the CAUSE as well as the object; but I am satisfied that every fair reader of these pages will instinctively know better. Miss Polly had simply selected the new guest, Mr. Starbuck, to show OTHERS, particularly Larry Hawkins, what she COULD do if she were inclined to be civil. For two days she "fixed up" her distracting hair at him so that its silken floss encircled her head like a nimbus; she tucked her oval chin into a white fichu instead of a buttonless collar; she appeared at dinner in a newly starched yellow frock! She talked to him with "company manners;" said she would "admire to go to San Francisco," and asked if he knew her old friends the Fauquier girls from "Faginia." The colonel was somewhat disturbed; he was glad that his daughter had become less negligent of her personal appearance; he could not but see, with the others, how it enhanced her graces; but he was, with the others, not entirely satisfied with her reasons. And he could not help observing--what was more or less patent to ALL--that Starbuck was far from being equally responsive to her attentions, and at times was indifferent and almost uncivil. Nobody seemed to be satisfied with Polly's transformation but herself.

But eventually she was obliged to assert herself. The third evening after Starbuck's arrival she was going over to the cabin of Aunt Chloe, who not only did the washing for Buena Vista, but assisted Polly in dressmaking. It was not far, and the night was moonlit. As she crossed the garden she saw Starbuck moving in the manzanita bushes beyond; a mischievous light came into her eyes; she had not EXPECTED to meet him, but she had seen him go out, and there were always POSSIBILITIES. To her surprise, however, he merely lifted his hat as she passed, and turned abruptly in another direction. This was more than the little heart-breaker of Buena Vista was accustomed to!

"Oh, Mr. Starbuck!" she called, in her laziest voice.

He turned almost impatiently.

"Since you're so civil and pressing, I thought I'd tell you I was just runnin' over to Aunt Chloe's," she said dryly.

"I should think it was hardly the proper thing for a young lady to do at this time of night," he said superciliously. "But you know best,--you know the people here."

Polly's cheeks and eyes flamed. "Yes, I reckon I do," she said crisply; "it's only a

STRANGER here would think of being rude. Good-night, Mr. Starbuck!"

She tripped away after this Parthian shot, yet feeling, even in her triumph, that the conceited fool seemed actually relieved at her departure! And for the first time she now thought that she had seen something in his face that she did not like! But her lazy independence reasserted itself soon, and half an hour later, when she had left Aunt Chloe's cabin, she had regained her self-esteem. Yet, to avoid meeting him again, she took a longer route home, across the dried ditch and over the bluff, scarred by hydraulics, and so fell, presently, upon the old garden at the point where it adjoined the abandoned diggings. She was quite sure she had escaped a meeting with Starbuck, and was gliding along under the shadow of the pear-trees, when she suddenly stopped. An indescribable terror overcame her as she stared at a spot in the garden, perfectly illuminated by the moonlight not fifty yards from where she stood. For she saw on its surface a human head--a man's head!--seemingly on the level of the ground, staring in her direction. A hysterical laugh sprang from her lips, and she caught at the branches above her or she would have fallen! Yet in that moment the head had vanished! The moonlight revealed the empty garden,--the ground she had gazed at,--but nothing more!

She had never been superstitious. As a child she had heard the negroes talk of "the hants,"--that is, "the HAUNTS" or spirits,--but had believed it a part of their ignorance, and unworthy a white child,--the daughter of their master! She had laughed with Dick Ruggles over the illusions of Larry, and had shared her father's contemptuous disbelief of the wandering visitant being anything but a living man; yet she would have screamed for assistance now, only for the greater fear of making her weakness known to Mr. Starbuck, and being dependent upon him for help. And with it came the sudden conviction that HE had seen this awful vision, too. This would account for his impatience of her presence and his rudeness. She felt faint and giddy. Yet after the first shock had passed, her old independence and pride came to her relief. She would go to the spot and examine it. If it were some trick or illusion, she would show her superiority and have the laugh on Starbuck. She set her white teeth, clenched her little hands, and started out into the moonlight. But alas! for women's weakness. The next moment she uttered a scream and almost fell into the arms of Mr. Starbuck, who had stepped out of the shadows beside her.

"So you see you HAVE been frightened," he said, with a strange, forced laugh;

"but I warned you about going out alone!"

Even in her fright she could not help seeing that he, too, seemed pale and agitated, at which she recovered her tongue and her self-possession.

"Anybody would be frightened by being dogged about under the trees," she said pertly.

"But you called out before you saw me," he said bluntly, "as if something had frightened you. That was WHY I came towards you."

She knew it was the truth; but as she would not confess to her vision, she fibbed outrageously.

"Frightened," she said, with pale but lofty indignation. "What was there to frighten me? I'm not a baby, to think I see a bogie in the dark!" This was said in the faint hope that HE had seen something too. If it had been Larry or her father who had met her, she would have confessed everything.

"You had better go in," he said curtly. "I will see you safe inside the house."

She demurred at this, but as she could not persist in her first bold intention of examining the locality of the vision without admitting its existence, she permitted him to walk with her to the house, and then at once fled to her own room. Larry and her father noticed their entrance together and their agitated manner, and were uneasy. Yet the colonel's paternal pride and Larry's lover's respect kept the two men from communicating their thoughts to each other.

"The confounded pup has been tryin' to be familiar, and Polly's set him down," thought Larry, with glowing satisfaction.

"He's been trying some of his sanctimonious Yankee abolition talk on Polly, and she shocked him!" thought the colonel exultingly.

But poor Polly had other things to think of in the silence of her room. Another woman would have unburdened herself to a confidante; but Polly was too loyal to her father to shatter his beliefs, and too high-spirited to take another and a lesser person into her confidence. She was certain that Aunt Chloe would be full of sympathetic belief and speculations, but she would not trust a nigger with what she couldn't tell her own father. For Polly really and truly believed that she had seen a ghost, no doubt the ghost of the murdered Sobriente, according to Larry's story. WHY he should appear with only his head above ground puzzled her, although it suggested the Catholic idea of purgatory, and he was a Catholic! Perhaps he would have risen entirely but for that stupid Starbuck's presence; perhaps he had a message for HER alone. The idea pleased Polly, albeit it was a "fearful joy" and attended with some cold shivering. Naturally, as a gentleman, he would appear to HER-- the daughter of a gentleman--the successor to his house--rather than to a Yankee stranger. What was she to do? For once her calm nerves were strangely thrilled; she could not think of undressing and going to bed, and two o'clock surprised her, still meditating, and occasionally peeping from her window upon the moonlit but vacant garden. If she saw him again, would she dare to go down alone? Suddenly she started to her feet with a beating heart! There was the unmistakable sound of a stealthy footstep in the passage, coming towards her room. Was it he? In spite of her high resolves she felt that if the door opened she should scream! She held her breath--the footsteps came nearer--were before her door--and PASSED!

Then it was that the blood rushed back to her cheek with a flush of indignation. Her room was at the end of the passage; there was nothing beyond but a private staircase, long disused, except by herself, as a short cut through the old patio to the garden. No one else knew of it, and no one else had the right of access to it! This insolent human intrusion--as she was satisfied it was now--overcame her fear, and she glided to the door. Opening it softly, she could hear the stealthy footsteps descending. She darted back, threw a shawl over her head and shoulders, and taking the small Derringer pistol which it had always been part of her ostentatious independence to place at her bed-head, she as stealthily followed the intruder. But the footsteps had died away before she reached the patio, and she saw only the small deserted, grass-grown courtyard, half hidden in shadows, in whose centre stood the fateful and long sealed-up well! A shudder came over her at again being brought into contact with the cause of her frightful vision, but as her eyes became accustomed to the darkness, she saw something more real and appalling! The well was no longer sealed! Fragments of bricks and boards lay around it! One end of a rope, coiled around it like a huge snake, descended its foul depths; and as she gazed with staring eyes, the head and shoulders of a man emerged slowly from it! But it was NOT the ghostly apparition of last evening, and her terror changed to scorn and indignation as she recognized the face of Starbuck!

Their eyes met; an oath broke from his lips. He made a movement to spring from the well, but as the girl started back, the pistol held in her hand was discharged aimlessly in the air, and the report echoed throughout the courtyard. With a curse Starbuck drew back, instantly disappeared in the well, and Polly fell fainting on the steps. When she came to, her father and Larry were at her side. They had been alarmed at the report, and had rushed quickly to the patio, but not in time to prevent the escape of Starbuck and his accomplice. By the time she had recovered her consciousness, they had learned the full extent of that extraordinary revelation which she had so innocently precipitated. Sobriente's well had really concealed a rich gold ledge,--actually tunneled and galleried by him secretly in the past,--and its only other outlet was an opening in the garden hidden by a stone which turned on a swivel. Its existence had been unknown to Sobriente's successor, but was known to the Kanaka who had worked with Sobriente, who fled with his daughter after the murder, but who no doubt was afraid to return and work the mine. He had imparted the secret to Starbuck, another half-breed, son of a Yankee missionary and Hawaiian wife, who had evidently conceived this plan of seeking Buena Vista with an accomplice, and secretly removing such gold as was still accessible. The accomplice, afterwards identified by Larry as the wandering tramp, failed to discover the secret entrance FROM the garden, and Starbuck was consequently obliged to attempt it from the hotel--for which purpose he had introduced himself as a boarder--by opening the disused well secretly at night. These facts were obtained from papers found in the otherwise valueless trunks, weighted with stones for ballast, which Starbuck had brought to the hotel to take away his stolen treasure in, but which he was obliged to leave in his hurried flight. The attempt would have doubtless succeeded but for Polly's courageous and timely interference!

And now that they had told her ALL, they only wanted to know what had first excited HER suspicions, and driven her to seek the well as the object of Starbuck's machinations? THEY had noticed her manner when she entered the house that night, and Starbuck's evident annoyance. Had she taxed him with her suspicions, and so discovered a clue?

It was a terrible temptation to Polly to pose as a more perfect heroine, and one may not blame her if she did not rise entirely superior to it. Her previous belief, that the head of the accomplice at the opening of the garden was that of a GHOST, she now felt was certainly in the way, as was also her conduct to Starbuck, whom she believed to be equally frightened, and whom she never once suspected! So she said, with a certain lofty simplicity, that there were SOME THINGS which she really did not care to talk about, and Larry and her father left her that night with the firm conviction that the rascal Starbuck had tried to tempt her to fly with him and his riches, and had been crushingly foiled. Polly never denied this, and once, in later days, when admiringly taxed with it by Larry, she admitted with dove-like simplicity that she MAY have been too foolishly polite to her father's guest for the sake of her father's hotel.

However, all this was of small account to the thrilling news of a new discovery and working of the "old gold ledge" at Buena Vista! As the three kept their secret from the world, the discovery was accepted in the neighborhood as the result of careful examination and prospecting on the part of Colonel Swinger and his partner Larry Hawkins. And when the latter gentleman afterwards boldly proposed to Polly Swinger, she mischievously declared that she accepted him only that the secret might not go "out of the family."

LIBERTY JONES'S DISCOVERY

It was at best merely a rocky trail winding along a shelf of the eastern slope of the Santa Cruz range, yet the only road between the sea and the inland valley. The hoof-prints of a whole century of zigzagging mules were impressed on the soil, regularly soaked by winter rains and dried by summer suns during that period; the occasional ruts of heavy, rude, wooden wheels--long obsolete--were still preserved and visible. Weather-worn boulders and ledges, lying in the unclouded glare of an August sky, radiated a quivering heat that was intolerable, even while above them the masts of gigantic pines rocked their tops in the cold southwestern trades from the unseen ocean beyond. A red, burning dust lay everywhere, as if the heat were slowly and visibly precipitating itself.

The creaking of wheels and axles, the muffled plunge of hoofs, and the cough of a horse in the dust thus stirred presently broke the profound woodland silence. Then a dirty white canvas-covered emigrant wagon slowly arose with the dust along the ascent. It was travel-stained and worn, and with its rawboned horses seemed to have reached the last stage of its journey and fitness. The only occupants, a man and a girl, appeared to be equally jaded and exhausted, with the added querulousness of discontent in their sallow and badly nourished faces. Their voices, too, were not unlike the creaking they had been pitched to overcome, and there was an absence of reserve and consciousness in their speech, which told pathetically of an equal absence of society.

"It's no user talkin'! I tell ye, ye hain't got no more sense than a coyote! I'm sick and tired of it, doggoned if I ain't! Ye ain't no more use nor a hossfly,--and jest ez hinderin'! It was along o' you that we lost the stock at Laramie, and ef ye'd bin at all decent and takin', we'd hev had kempany that helped, instead of laggin' on yere alone!"

"What did ye bring me for?" retorted the girl shrilly. "I might hev stayed with Aunt Marty. I wasn't hankerin' to come."

"Bring ye for?" repeated her father contemptuously; "I reckoned ye might he o' some account here, whar wimmin folks is skeerce, in the way o' helpin',--and mebbe gettin' yer married to some likely feller. Mighty much chance o' that, with yer yaller face and skin and bones."

"Ye can't blame me for takin' arter you, dad," she said, with a shrill laugh, but no other resentment of his brutality.

"Ye want somebody to take arter you--with a club," he retorted angrily. "Ye hear! Wot's that ye're doin' now?"

She had risen and walked to the tail of the wagon. "Goin' to get out and walk. I'm tired o' bein' jawed at."

She jumped into the road. The act was neither indignant nor vengeful; the frequency of such scenes had blunted their sting. She was probably "tired" of the quarrel, and ended it rudely. Her father, however, let fly a Parthian arrow.

"Ye needn't think I'm goin' to wait for ye, ez I hev! Ye've got to keep tetch with the team, or get left. And a good riddance of bad rubbidge."

In reply the girl dived into the underwood beside the trail, picked a wild berry or two, stripped a wand of young hazel she had broken off, and switching it at her side, skipped along on the outskirts of the wood and ambled after the wagon. Seen in the full, merciless glare of a Californian sky, she justified her father's description; thin and bony, her lank frame outstripped the body of her ragged calico dress, which was only kept on her shoulders by straps,--possibly her father's cast-off braces. A boy's soft felt hat covered her head, and shadowed her only notable feature, a pair of large dark eyes, looking larger for the hollow temples which narrowed the frame in which they were set.

So long as the wagon crawled up the ascent the girl knew she could easily keep up with it, or even distance the tired horses. She made one or two incursions into the wood, returning like an animal from quest of food, with something in her mouth, which she was tentatively chewing, and once only with some inedible mandrono berries, plucked solely for their brilliant coloring. It was very hot and singularly close; the higher current of air had subsided, and, looking up, a singular haze seemed to have taken its place between the treetops. Suddenly she heard a strange, rumbling sound; an odd giddiness overtook her, and she was obliged to clutch at a sapling to support herself; she laughed vacantly, though a little frightened, and looked vaguely towards the summit of the road; but the wagon had already disappeared. A strange feeling of nausea then overcame her; she spat out the leaves she had been chewing, disgustedly. But the sensation as quickly passed, and she once more sought the trail and began slowly to follow the tracks of the wagon. The air blew freshly, the treetops began again to rock over her head, and the incident was forgotten.

Presently she paused; she must have missed the trail, for the wagon tracks had ended abruptly before a large boulder that lay across the mountain trail. She dipped into the woods again; here there were other wagon tracks that confused her. It was like her dogged, stupid father to miss the trail; she felt a gleam of malicious satisfaction at his discomfiture. Sooner or later, he would have to retrace his steps and virtually come back for her! She took up a position where two rough wheel ruts and tracks intersected each other, one of which must be the missing trail. She noticed, too, the broader hoof-prints of cattle without the following wheel ruts, and instead of traces, the long smooth trails made by the dragging of logs, and knew by these tokens that she must be near the highway or some woodman's hut or ranch. She began to be thirsty, and was glad, presently, when her quick, rustic ear caught the tinkling of water. Yet it was not so easy to discover, and she was getting footsore and tired again before she found it, some distance away, in a gully coming from a fissure in a dislocated piece of outcrop. It was beautifully clear, cold, and sparkling, with a slightly sweetish taste, yet unlike the brackish "alkali" of the plains. It refreshed and soothed her greatly, so much that, reclining against a tree, but where she would be quite visible from the trail, her eyes closed dreamily, and presently she slept.

When she awoke, the shafts of sunlight were striking almost level into her eyes. She must have slept two hours. Her father had not returned; she knew the passage of the wagon would have awakened her. She began to feel strange, but not yet alarmed; it was only the uncertainty that made her uneasy. Had her father really gone on by some other trail? Or had he really hurried on and left her, as he said he would? The thought brought an odd excitement to her rather than any fear. A sudden sense of freedom, as if some galling chain had dropped from her, sent a singular thrill through her frame. Yet she felt confused with her independence, not knowing what to do with it, and momentarily dazzled with the possible gift.

At this moment she heard voices, and the figures of two men appeared on the trail.

They were talking earnestly, and walking as if familiar with the spot, yet gazing around them as if at some novelty of the aspect.

"And look there," said one; "there has been some serious disturbance of that outcrop," pointing in the direction of the spring; "the lower part has distinctly subsided." He spoke with a certain authority, and dominance of position, and was evidently the superior, as he was the elder of the two, although both were roughly dressed.

"Yes, it does kinder look as if it had lost its holt, like the ledge yonder."

"And you see I am right; the movement was from east to west," continued the elder man.

The girl could not comprehend what they said, and even thought them a little silly. But she advanced towards them; at which they stopped short, staring at her. With feminine instinct she addressed the more important one:--

"Ye ain't passed no wagon nor team goin' on, hev ye?"

"What sort of wagon?" said the man.

"Em'grant wagon, two yaller hosses. Old man--my dad--drivin'." She added the latter kinship as a protecting influence against strangers, in spite of her previous independence.

The men glanced at each other.

"How long ago?"

The girl suddenly remembered that she had slept two hours.

"Sens noon," she said hesitatingly.

"Since the earthquake?"

"Wot's that?"

The man came impatiently towards her. "How did you come here?"

"Got outer the wagon to walk. I reckon dad missed the trail, and hez got off somewhere where I can't find him."

"What trail was he on,--where was he going?"

"Sank Hozay,* I reckon. He was goin' up the grade--side o' the hill; he must hev turned off where there's a big rock hangin' over."

* San Jose.

"Did you SEE him turn off?"

"No."

The second man, who was in hearing distance, had turned away, and was ostentatiously examining the sky and the treetops; the man who had spoken to her joined him, and they said something in a low voice. They turned again and came slowly towards her. She, from some obscure sense of imitation, stared at the treetops and the sky as the second man had done. But the first man now laid his hand kindly on her shoulder and said, "Sit down."

Then they told her there had been an earthquake so strong that it had thrown down a part of the hillside, including the wagon trail. That a wagon team and driver, such as she had described, had been carried down with it, crushed to fragments, and buried under a hundred feet of rock in the gulch below. A party had gone down to examine, but it would be weeks perhaps before they found it, and she must be prepared for the worst. She looked at them vaguely and with tearless eyes.

"Then ye reckon dad's dead?"

"We fear it."

"Then wot's a-goin' to become o' me?" she said simply.

They glanced again at each other. "Have you no friends in California?" said the elder man.

"Nary one."

"What was your father going to do?"

"Dunno. I reckon HE didn't either."

"You may stay here for the present," said the elder man meditatively. "Can you milk?"

The girl nodded. "And I suppose you know something about looking after stock?" he continued.

The girl remembered that her father thought she didn't, but this was no time for criticism, and she again nodded.

"Come with me," said the older man, rising. "I suppose," he added, glancing at her ragged frock, "everything you have is in the wagon."

She nodded, adding with the same cold naivete, "It ain't much!"

They walked on, the girl following; at times straying furtively on either side, as if meditating an escape in the woods,--which indeed had once or twice been vaguely in her thoughts,--but chiefly to avoid further questioning and not to hear what the men said to each other. For they were evidently speaking of her, and she could not help hearing the younger repeat her words, "Wot's agoin' to become o' me?" with considerable amusement, and the addition: "She'll take care of herself, you bet! I call that remark o' hers the richest thing out."

"And I call the state of things that provoked it--monstrous!" said the elder man grimly. "You don't know the lives of these people."

Presently they came to an open clearing in the forest, yet so incomplete that many of the felled trees, partly lopped of their boughs, still lay where they had fallen. There was a cabin or dwelling of unplaned, unpainted boards; very simple in structure, yet made in a workmanlike fashion, quite unlike the usual log cabin she had seen. This made her think that the elder man was a "towny," and not a frontiersman like the other.

As they approached the cabin the elder man stopped, and turning to her, said:--

"Do you know Indians?"

The girl started, and then recovering herself with a quick laugh: "G'lang!--there ain't any Injins here!"

"Not the kind YOU mean; these are very peaceful. There's a squaw here whom you will"--he stopped, hesitated as he looked critically at the girl, and then corrected himself--"who will help you."

He pushed open the cabin door and showed an interior, equally simple but well joined and fitted,--a marvel of neatness and finish to the frontier girl's eye. There were shelves and cupboards and other conveniences, yet with no ostentation of refinement to frighten her rustic sensibilities.

Then he pushed open another door leading into a shed and called "Waya." A stout, undersized Indian woman, fitted with a coarse cotton gown, but cleaner and more presentable than the girl's one frock, appeared in the doorway. "This is Waya, who attends to the cooking and cleaning," he said; "and by the way, what is your name?"

"Libby Jones."

He took a small memorandum book and a "stub" of pencil from his pocket.

"Elizabeth Jones," he said, writing it down. The girl interposed a long red hand.

"No," she interrupted sharply, "not Elizabeth, but Libby, short for Lib'rty."

"Liberty?"

"Yes."

"Liberty Jones, then. Well, Waya, this is Miss Jones, who will look after the cows and calves--and the dairy." Then glancing at her torn dress, he added: "You'll find some clean things in there, until I can send up something from San Jose. Waya will show you."

Without further speech he turned away with the other man. When they were some distance from the cabin, the younger remarked:--

"More like a boy than a girl, ain't she?"

"So much the better for her work," returned the elder grimly.

"I reckon! I was only thinkin' she didn't han'some much either as a boy or girl, eh, doctor?" he pursued.

"Well! as THAT won't make much difference to the cows, calves, or the dairy, it needn't trouble US," returned the doctor dryly. But here a sudden outburst of laughter from the cabin made them both turn in that direction. They were in time to see Liberty Jones dancing out of the cabin door in a large cotton pinafore, evidently belonging to the squaw, who was following her with half-laughing, half-frightened expostulations. The two men stopped and gazed at the spectacle.

"Don't seem to be takin' the old man's death very pow'fully," said the younger, with a laugh.

"Quite as much as he deserved, I daresay," said the doctor curtly. "If the accident had happened to HER, he would have whined and whimpered to us for the sake of getting something, but have been as much relieved, you may be certain. SHE'S too young and too natural to be a hypocrite yet."

Suddenly the laughter ceased and Liberty Jones's voice arose, shrill but masterful: "Thar, that'll do! Quit now! You jest get back to your scrubbin'--d'ye hear? I'm boss o' this shanty, you bet!"

The doctor turned with a grim smile to his companion. "That's the only thing that bothered me, and I've been waiting for. She's settled it. She'll do. Come."

They turned away briskly through the wood. At the end of half an hour's walk they found the team that had brought them there in waiting, and drove towards

San Jose. It was nearly ten miles before they passed another habitation or trace of clearing. And by this time night had fallen upon the cabin they had left, and upon the newly made orphan and her Indian companion, alone and contented in that trackless solitude.

*****

Liberty Jones had been a year at the cabin. In that time she had learned that her employer's name was Doctor Ruysdael, that he had a lucrative practice in San Jose, but had also "taken up" a league or two of wild forest land in the Santa Cruz range, which he preserved and held after a fashion of his own, which gave him the reputation of being a "crank" among the very few neighbors his vast possessions permitted, and the equally few friends his singular tastes allowed him. It was believed that a man owning such an enormous quantity of timber land, who should refuse to set up a sawmill and absolutely forbid the felling of trees; who should decline to connect it with the highway to Santa Cruz, and close it against improvement and speculation, had given sufficient evidence of his insanity; but when to this was added the rumor that he himself was not only devoid of the human instinct of hunting the wild animals with which his domain abounded, but that he held it so sacred to their use as to forbid the firing of a gun within his limits, and that these restrictions were further preserved and "policed" by the scattered remnants of a band of aborigines,--known as "digger Injins,"--it was seriously hinted that his eccentricity had acquired a political and moral significance, and demanded legislative interference. But the doctor was a rich man, a necessity to his patients, a good marksman, and, it was rumored, did not include his fellow men among the animals he had a distaste for killing.

Of all this, however, Liberty knew little and cared less. The solitude appealed to her sense of freedom; she did not "hanker" after a society she had never known. At the end of the first week, when the doctor communicated to her briefly, by letter, the convincing proofs of the death of her father and his entombment beneath the sunken cliff, she accepted the fact without comment or apparent emotion. Two months later, when her only surviving relative, "Aunt Marty," of Missouri, acknowledged the news--communicated by Doctor Ruysdael--with Scriptural quotations and the cheerful hope that it "would be a lesson to her" and she would "profit in her new place," she left her aunt's letter unanswered.

She looked after the cows and calves with an interest that was almost possessory, patronized and played with the squaw,--yet made her feel her inferiority,--and moved among the peaceful aborigines with the domination of a white woman and a superior. She tolerated the half-monthly visits of "Jim Hoskins," the young companion of the doctor, who she learned was the doctor's factor and overseer of the property, who lived seven miles away on an agricultural clearing, and whose control of her actions was evidently limited by the doctor,--for the doctor's sake alone. Nor was Mr. Hoskins inclined to exceed those limits. He looked upon her as something abnormal,--a "crank" as remarkable in her way as her patron was in his, neuter of sex and vague of race, and he simply restricted his supervision to the bringing and taking of messages. She remained sole queen of the domain. A rare straggler from the main road, penetrating this seclusion, might have scarcely distinguished her from Waya, in her coarse cotton gown and slouched hat, except for the free stride which contrasted with her companion's waddle. Once, in following an estrayed calf, she had crossed the highway and been saluted by a passing teamster in the digger dialect; yet the mistake left no sting in her memory. And, like the digger, she shrank from that civilization which had only proved a hard taskmaster.

The sole touch of human interest she had in her surroundings was in the rare visits of the doctor and his brief but sincere commendation of her rude and rustic work. It is possible that the strange, middle-aged, gray-haired, intellectual man, whose very language was at times mysterious and unintelligible to her, and whose suggestion of power awed her, might have touched some untried filial chord in her being. Although she felt that, save for absolute freedom, she was little more to him than she had been to her father, yet he had never told her she had "no sense," that she was "a hindrance," and he had even praised her performance of her duties. Eagerly as she looked for his coming, in his actual presence she felt a singular uneasiness of which she was not entirely ashamed, and if she was relieved at his departure, it none the less left her to a delightful memory of him, a warm sense of his approval, and a fierce ambition to be worthy of it, for which she would have sacrificed herself or the other miserable retainers about her, as a matter of course.

She had driven Waya and the other squaws far along the sparse tableland pasture in search of missing stock; she herself had lain out all night on the rocks beside an ailing heifer. Yet, while satisfied to earn his praise for the performance of her duty, for some feminine reason she thought more frequently of a casual remark he had made on his last visit: "You are stronger and more healthy in this air," he had said, looking critically into her face. "We have got that abominable alkali out of your system, and wholesome food will do the rest." She was not sure she had quite understood him, but she remembered that she had felt her face grow hot when he spoke,--perhaps because she had not understood him.

His next visit was a day or two delayed, and in her anxiety she had ventured as far as the highway to earnestly watch for his coming. From her hiding-place in the underwood she could see the team and Jim Hoskins already waiting for him. Presently she saw him drive up to the trail in a carryall with a party of ladies and gentlemen. He alighted, bade "Good-by" to the party, and the team turned to retrace its course. But in that single moment she had been struck and bewildered by what seemed to her the dazzlingly beautiful apparel of the women, and their prettiness. She felt a sudden consciousness of her own coarse, shapeless calico gown, her straggling hair, and her felt hat, and a revulsion of feeling seized her. She crept like a wounded animal out of the underwood, and then ran swiftly and almost fiercely back towards the cabin. She ran so fast that for a time she almost kept pace with the doctor and Hoskins in the wagon on the distant trail. Then she dived into the underwood again, and making a short cut through the forest, came at the end of two hours within hailing distance of the cabin,--footsore and exhausted, in spite of the strange excitement that had driven her back. Here she thought she heard voices- his voice among the rest calling her, but the same singular revulsion of feeling hurried her vaguely on again, even while she experienced a foolish savage delight in not answering the summons. In this erratic wandering she came upon the spring she had found on her first entrance in the forest a year ago, and drank feverishly a second time at its trickling source. She could see that since her first visit it had worn a great hollow below the tree roots and now formed a shining, placid pool. As she stooped to look at it, she suddenly observed that it reflected her whole figure as in a cruel mirror,--her slouched hat and loosened hair, her coarse and shapeless gown, her hollow cheeks and dry yellow skin,--in all their hopeless, uncompromising details. She uttered a quick, angry, half-reproachful cry, and turned again to fly. But she had not gone far before she came upon the hurrying figures and anxious faces of the doctor and Hoskins. She stopped, trembling and irresolute.

"Ah," said the doctor, in a tone of frank relief. "Here you are! I was getting worried about you. Waya said you had been gone since morning!" He stopped and looked at her attentively. "Is anything the matter?"

His evident concern sent a warm glow over her chilly frame, and yet the strange sensation remained. "No--no!" she stammered.

Doctor Ruysdael turned to Hoskins. "Go back and tell Waya I've found her."

Libby felt that the doctor only wanted to get rid of his companion, and became awed again.

"Has anybody been bothering you?"

"No."

"Have the diggers frightened you?"

"No"--with a gesture of contempt.

"Have you and Waya quarreled?"

"Nary"--with a faint, tremulous smile.

He still stared at her, and then dropped his blue eyes musingly. "Are you lonely here? Would you rather go to San Jose?"

Like a flash the figures of the two smartly dressed women started up before her again, with every detail of their fresh and wholesome finery as cruelly distinct as had been her own shapeless ugliness in the mirror of the spring. "No! NO!" she broke out vehemently and passionately. "Never!"

He smiled gently. "Look here! I'll send you up some books. You read--don't you?" She nodded quickly. "Some magazines and papers. Odd I never thought of it before," he added half musingly. "Come along to the cabin. And," he stopped again and said decisively, "the next time you want anything, don't wait for me to come, but write."

A few days after he left she received a package of books,--an odd collection of novels, magazines, and illustrated journals of the period. She received them eagerly as an evidence of his concern for her, but it is to be feared that her youthful nature found little satisfaction in the gratification of fancy. Many of the people she read of were strange to her; many of the incidents related seemed to her mere lies; some tales which treated of people in her own sphere she found profoundly uninteresting. In one of the cheaper magazines she chanced upon a fashion plate; she glanced eagerly through all the others for a like revelation until she got a dozen together, when she promptly relegated the remaining literature to a corner and oblivion. The text accompanying the plates was in a jargon not always clear, but her instinct supplied the rest. She dispatched by Hoskins a note to Doctor Ruysdael: "Please send me some brite kalikers and things for sewing. You told me to ask." A few days later brought the response in a good-sized parcel.

Yet this did not keep her from her care of the stock nor her rambles in the forest; she was quick to utilize her rediscovery of the spring for watering the cattle; it was not so far afield as the half-dried creek in the canyon, and was a quiet sylvan spot. She ate her frugal midday meal there and drank of its waters, and, secure in her seclusion, bathed there and made her rude toilet when the cows were driven home. But she did not again look into its mirrored surface when it was tranquil!

And so a month passed. But when Doctor Ruysdael was again due at the cabin, a letter was brought by Hoskins, with the news that he was called away on professional business down the coast, and could not come until two weeks later. In the disappointment that overcame her, she did not at first notice that Hoskins was gazing at her with a singular expression, which was really one of undisguised admiration. Never having seen this before in the eyes of any man who looked at her, she referred it to some vague "larking" or jocularity, for which she was in no mood.

"Say, Libby! you're gettin' to be a right smart-lookin' gal. Seems to agree with ye up here," said Hoskins with an awkward laugh. "Darned ef ye ain't lookin' awful purty!"

"G'long!" said Liberty Jones, more than ever convinced of his badinage.

"Fact," said Hoskins energetically. "Why, Doc would tell ye so, too. See ef he don't!"

At this Liberty Jones felt her face grow hot. "You jess get!" she said, turning away in as much embarrassment as anger. Yet he hovered near her with awkward attentions that pleased while it still angered her. He offered to go with her to look up the cows; she flatly declined, yet with a strange satisfaction in his evident embarrassment. This may have lent some animation to her face, for he drew a long breath and said:--

"Don't go pertendin' ye don't know yer purty. Say, let me and you walk a bit and have a talk together." But Libby had another idea in her mind and curtly dismissed him. Then she ran swiftly to the spring, for the words "The Doc will tell ye so, too" were ringing in her ears. The doctor who came with the two beautifully dressed women! HE--would tell her she was pretty! She had not dared to look at herself in that crystal mirror since that dreadful day two months ago. She would now.

It was a pretty place in the cool shade of the giant trees, and the hoof-marks of cattle drinking from the run beneath the pool had not disturbed the margin of that tranquil sylvan basin. For a moment she stood tremulous and uncertain, and then going up to the shining mirror, dropped on her knees before it with her thin red hands clasped on her lap. Unconsciously she had taken the attitude of prayer; perhaps there was something like it in her mind.

And then the light glanced full on the figure that she saw there!

It fell on a full oval face and throat guileless of fleck or stain, smooth as a child's and glowing with health; on large dark eyes, no longer sunk in their orbits, but filled with an eager, happy light; on bared arms now shapely in contour and cushioned with firm flesh; on a dazzling smile, the like of which had never been on the face of Liberty Jones before!

She rose to her feet, and yet lingered as if loath to part from this delightful vision. Then a fear overcame her that it was some trick of the water, and she sped swiftly back to the house to consult the little mirror which hung in her sleeping-room, but which she had never glanced at since the momentous day of the spring. She took it shyly into the sunshine, and found that it corroborated the reflection of the spring. That night she worked until late at the calico Doctor Ruysdael had sent her, and went to bed happy. The next day brought her Hoskins again with a feeble excuse of inquiring if she had a letter for the doctor, and she was surprised to find that he was reinforced by a stranger from Hoskins's farm, who was equally awkward and vaguely admiring. But the appearance of the TWO men produced a singular phase in her impressions and experience. She was no longer indignant at Hoskins, but she found relief in accepting the compliments of the stranger in preference, and felt a delight in Hoskins's discomfiture. Waya, promoted to the burlesque of a chaperone, grinned with infinite delight and understanding.

When at last the day came for the doctor's arrival, he was duly met by Hoskins, and as duly informed by that impressible subordinate of the great change in Liberty's appearance. But the doctor was far from being equally impressed with his factor's story, and indeed showed much more interest in the appearance of the stock which they met along the road. Once the doctor got out of the wagon to inspect a cow, and particularly the coat of a rough draught horse that had been turned out and put under Liberty's care. "His skin is like velvet," said the doctor. "The girl evidently understands stock, and knows how to keep them in condition."

"I reckon she's beginning to understand herself, too," said Hoskins. "Golly! wait till ye see HER."

The doctor DID see her, but with what feelings he did not as frankly express. She was not at the cabin when they arrived, but presently appeared from the direction of the spring where, for reasons of her own, she had evidently made her toilet. Doctor Ruysdael was astounded; Hoskins's praise was not exaggerated; and there was an added charm that Hoskins was not prepared for. She had put on a gown of her own making,--the secret toil of many a long night,--amateurishly fashioned from some cheap yellow calico the doctor had sent her, yet fitting her wonderfully, and showing every curve of her graceful figure. Unaccented by a corset,--an article she had never known,--even the lines of the stiff, unyielding calico had a fashion that was nymph-like and suited her unfettered limbs. Doctor Ruysdael was profoundly moved. Though a philosopher, he was practical. He found himself suddenly confronted not only by a beautiful girl, but a problem! It was impossible to keep the existence of this woodland nymph from the knowledge of his distant neighbors; it was equally impossible for him to assume the responsibility of keeping a goddess like this in her present position. He had noticed her previous improvement, but had never dreamed that pure and wholesome living could in two months work such a miracle. And he was to a certain degree responsible, HE had created her,--a beautiful Frankenstein, whose lustrous, appealing eyes were even now menacing his security and position.

Perhaps she saw trouble and perplexity in the face where she had expected admiration and pleasure, for a slight chill went over her as he quickly praised the appearance of the stock and spoke of her own improvement. But when they were alone, he turned to her abruptly.

"You said you had no wish to go to San Jose?"

"No." Yet she was conscious that her greatest objection had been removed, and she colored faintly.

"Listen to me," he said dryly. "You deserve a better position than this,--a better home and surroundings than you have here. You are older, too,--a woman almost,--and you must look ahead."

A look of mingled fright, reproach, and appeal came into her eloquent face. "Yer wantin' to send me away?" she stammered.

"No," he said frankly. "It is you who are GROWING away. This is no longer the place for you."

"But I want to stay. I don't wanter go. I am--I WAS happy here."

"But I'm thinking of giving up this place. It takes up too much of my time. You must be provided"--

"YOU are going away?" she said passionately.

"Yes."

"Take me with you. I'll go anywhere!--to San Jose---wherever you go. Don't turn me off as dad did, for I'll foller you as I never followed dad. I'll go with you--or I'll die!"

There was neither fear nor shame in her words; it was the outspoken instinct of the animal he had been rearing; he was convinced and appalled by it.

"I am returning to San Jose at once," he said gravely. "You shall go with me--FOR THE PRESENT! Get yourself ready!"

He took her to San Jose, and temporarily to the house of a patient,--a widow lady,--while he tried, alone, to grapple with the problem that now confronted him. But that problem became more complicated at the end of the third day, by Liberty Jones falling suddenly and alarmingly ill. The symptoms were so grave that the doctor, in his anxiety, called in a brother physician in consultation. When the examination was over, the two men withdrew and stared at each other.

"Of course there is no doubt that the symptoms all point to slow arsenical poisoning," said the consulting doctor.

"Yes," said Ruysdael quickly, "yet it is utterly inexplicable, both as to motive and opportunity."

"Humph!" said the other grimly, "young ladies take arsenic in minute doses to improve the complexion and promote tissue, forgetting that the effects are cumulative when they stop suddenly. Your young friend has 'sworn off' too quickly."

"But it is impossible," said Doctor Ruysdael impatiently. "She is a mere child--a country girl--ignorant of such habits."

"Humph! the peasants in the Tyrol try it on themselves after noticing the effect on the coats of cattle."

Doctor Ruysdael started. A recollection of the sleek draught horse flashed upon him. He rose and hastily re-entered the patient's room. In a few moments he returned. "Do you think I could remove her at once to the mountains?" he said gravely.

"Yes, with care and a return to graduated doses of the same poison; you know it's the only remedy just now," answered the other.

By noon the next day the doctor and his patient had returned to the cabin, but Ruysdael himself carried the helpless Liberty Jones to the spring and deposited her gently beside it. "You may drink now," he said gravely.

The girl did so eagerly, apparently imbibing new strength from the sparkling water. The doctor meanwhile coolly filled a phial from the same source, and made a hasty test of the contents by the aid of some other phials from his case. The result seemed to satisfy him. Then he said gravely:

"And THIS is the spring you had discovered?"

The girl nodded.

"And you and the cattle have daily used it?"

She nodded again wonderingly. Then she caught his hand appealingly.

"You won't send me away?"

He smiled oddly as he glanced from the waters of the hill to the brimming eyes. "No."

"No-r," tremulously, "go away--yourself?"

The doctor looked this time only into her eyes. There was a tremendous idea in his own, which seemed in some way to have solved that dreadful problem.

"No! We will stay here TOGETHER."

*****

Six months later there was a paragraph in the San Francisco press: "The wonderful Arsenical Spring in the Santa Cruz Mountain, known as 'Liberty Spring,' discovered by Doctor Ruysdael, has proved such a remarkable success that we understand the temporary huts for patients are to be shortly replaced by a magnificent Spa Hotel worthy of the spot, and the eligible villa sites it has brought into the market. It will be a source of pleasure to all to know that the beautiful nymph--a worthy successor to the far-famed 'Elise' of the German 'Brunnen'--who has administered the waters to so many grateful patients will still be in attendance, although it is rumored that she is shortly to become the wife of the distinguished discoverer."

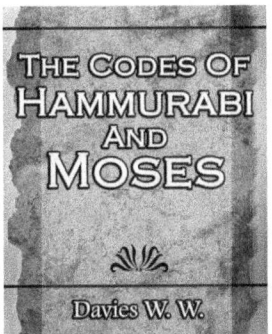

The Codes Of Hammurabi And Moses
W. W. Davies

QTY

The discovery of the Hammurabi Code is one of the greatest achievements of archaeology, and is of paramount interest, not only to the student of the Bible, but also to all those interested in ancient history...

Religion   **ISBN:** *1-59462-338-4*   **Pages:132**
MSRP $12.95

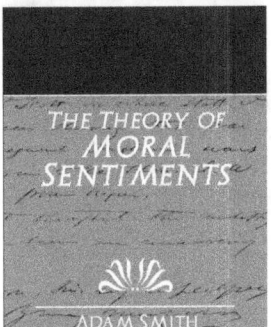

The Theory of Moral Sentiments
Adam Smith

QTY

This work from 1749. contains original theories of conscience amd moral judgment and it is the foundation for systemof morals.

Philosophy ISBN: *1-59462-777-0*   **Pages:536**
MSRP $19.95

Jessica's First Prayer
Hesba Stretton

QTY

In a screened and secluded corner of one of the many railway-bridges which span the streets of London there could be seen a few years ago, from five o'clock every morning until half past eight, a tidily set-out coffee-stall, consisting of a trestle and board, upon which stood two large tin cans, with a small fire of charcoal burning under each so as to keep the coffee boiling during the early hours of the morning when the work-people were thronging into the city on their way to their daily toil...

Pages:84

Childrens   ISBN: *1-59462-373-2*   *MSRP $9.95*

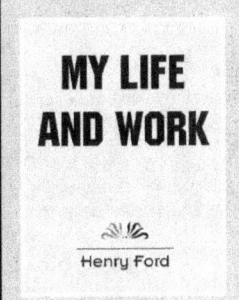

My Life and Work
Henry Ford

QTY

Henry Ford revolutionized the world with his implementation of mass production for the Model T automobile. Gain valuable business insight into his life and work with his own auto-biography... "We have only started on our development of our country we have not as yet, with all our talk of wonderful progress, done more than scratch the surface. The progress has been wonderful enough but..."

Pages:300

Biographies/   **ISBN:** *1-59462-198-5*   *MSRP $21.95*

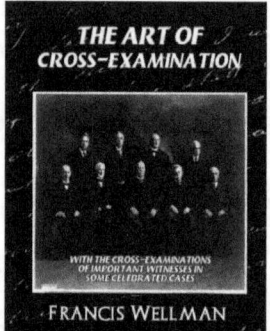

The Art of Cross-Examination
Francis Wellman

QTY

I presume it is the experience of every author, after his first book is published upon an important subject, to be almost overwhelmed with a wealth of ideas and illustrations which could readily have been included in his book, and which to his own mind, at least, seem to make a second edition inevitable. Such certainly was the case with me; and when the first edition had reached its sixth impression in five months, I rejoiced to learn that it seemed to my publishers that the book had met with a sufficiently favorable reception to justify a second and considerably enlarged edition. ..

Reference   ISBN: *1-59462-647-2*

Pages:412

MSRP $19.95

On the Duty of Civil Disobedience
Henry David Thoreau

QTY

Thoreau wrote his famous essay, On the Duty of Civil Disobedience, as a protest against an unjust but popular war and the immoral but popular institution of slave-owning. He did more than write—he declined to pay his taxes, and was hauled off to gaol in consequence. Who can say how much this refusal of his hastened the end of the war and of slavery ?

Law   ISBN: *1-59462-747-9*

Pages:48

MSRP $7.45

Dream Psychology Psychoanalysis for Beginners
Sigmund Freud

QTY

Sigmund Freud, born Sigismund Schlomo Freud (May 6, 1856 - September 23, 1939), was a Jewish-Austrian neurologist and psychiatrist who co-founded the psychoanalytic school of psychology. Freud is best known for his theories of the unconscious mind, especially involving the mechanism of repression; his redefinition of sexual desire as mobile and directed towards a wide variety of objects; and his therapeutic techniques, especially his understanding of transference in the therapeutic relationship and the presumed value of dreams as sources of insight into unconscious desires.

Dream Psychology
Psychoanalysis for Beginners

Sigmund Freud

Psychology   ISBN: *1-59462-905-6*

Pages:196

MSRP $15.45

The Miracle of Right Thought
Orison Swett Marden

QTY

Believe with all of your heart that you will do what you were made to do. When the mind has once formed the habit of holding cheerful, happy, prosperous pictures, it will not be easy to form the opposite habit. It does not matter how improbable or how far away this realization may see, or how dark the prospects may be, if we visualize them as best we can, as vividly as possible, hold tenaciously to them and vigorously struggle to attain them, they will gradually become actualized, realized in the life. But a desire, a longing without endeavor, a yearning abandoned or held indifferently will vanish without realization.

Pages:360

Self Help   ISBN: *1-59462-644-8*

MSRP $25.45

The Rosicrucian Cosmo-Conception Mystic Christianity *by Max Heindel*   ISBN: *1-59462-188-8*   **$38.95**
The Rosicrucian Cosmo-conception is not dogmatic, neither does it appeal to any other authority than the reason of the student. It is: not controversial, but is: sent forth in the, hope that it may help to clear...   New Age/Religion Pages 646

Abandonment To Divine Providence *by Jean-Pierre de Caussade*   ISBN: *1-59462-228-0*   **$25.95**
"The Rev. Jean Pierre de Caussade was one of the most remarkable spiritual writers of the Society of Jesus in France in the 18th Century. His death took place at Toulouse in 1751. His works have gone through many editions and have been republished...   Inspirational/Religion Pages 400

Mental Chemistry *by Charles Haanel*   ISBN: *1-59462-192-6*   **$23.95**
Mental Chemistry allows the change of material conditions by combining and appropriately utilizing the power of the mind. Much like applied chemistry creates something new and unique out of careful combinations of chemicals the mastery of mental chemistry...   New Age Pages 354

The Letters of Robert Browning and Elizabeth Barret Barrett 1845-1846 vol II   ISBN: *1-59462-193-4*   **$35.95**
by Robert Browning and Elizabeth Barrett   Biographies Pages 596

Gleanings In Genesis (volume I) *by Arthur W. Pink*   ISBN: *1-59462-130-6*   **$27.45**
Appropriately has Genesis been termed "the seed plot of the Bible" for in it we have, in germ form, almost all of the great doctrines which are afterwards fully developed in the books of Scripture which follow...   Religion/Inspirational Pages 420

The Master Key *by L. W. de Laurence*   ISBN: *1-59462-001-6*   **$30.95**
In no branch of human knowledge has there been a more lively increase of the spirit of research during the past few years than in the study of Psychology, Concentration and Mental Discipline. The requests for authentic lessons in Thought Control, Mental Discipline and...   New Age/Business Pages 422

The Lesser Key Of Solomon Goetia *by L. W. de Laurence*   ISBN: *1-59462-092-X*   **$9.95**
This translation of the first book of the "Lernegton" which is now for the first time made accessible to students of Talismanic Magic was done, after careful collation and edition, from numerous Ancient Manuscripts in Hebrew, Latin, and French...   New Age/Occult Pages 92

Rubaiyat Of Omar Khayyam *by Edward Fitzgerald*   ISBN:*1-59462-332-5*   **$13.95**
Edward Fitzgerald, whom the world has already learned, in spite of his own efforts to remain within the shadow of anonymity, to look upon as one of the rarest poets of the century, was born at Bredfield, in Suffolk, on the 31st of March, 1809. He was the third son of John Purcell...   Music Pages 172

Ancient Law *by Henry Maine*   ISBN: *1-59462-128-4*   **$29.95**
The chief object of the following pages is to indicate some of the earliest ideas of mankind, as they are reflected in Ancient Law, and to point out the relation of those ideas to modern thought.   Religiom/History Pages 452

Far-Away Stories *by William J. Locke*   ISBN: *1-59462-129-2*   **$19.45**
"Good wine needs no bush, but a collection of mixed vintages does. And this book is just such a collection. Some of the stories I do not want to remain buried for ever in the museum files of dead magazine-numbers an author's not unpardonable vanity..."   Fiction Pages 272

Life of David Crockett *by David Crockett*   ISBN: *1-59462-250-7*   **$27.45**
"Colonel David Crockett was one of the most remarkable men of the times in which he lived. Born in humble life, but gifted with a strong will, an indomitable courage, and unremitting perseverance...   Biographies/New Age Pages 424

Lip-Reading *by Edward Nitchie*   ISBN: *1-59462-206-X*   **$25.95**
Edward B. Nitchie, founder of the New York School for the Hard of Hearing, now the Nitchie School of Lip-Reading, Inc, wrote "LIP-READING Principles and Practice". The development and perfecting of this meritorious work on lip-reading was an undertaking...   How-to Pages 400

A Handbook of Suggestive Therapeutics, Applied Hypnotism, Psychic Science   ISBN: *1-59462-214-0*   **$24.95**
by Henry Munro   Health/New Age/Health/Self-help Pages 376

A Doll's House: and Two Other Plays *by Henrik Ibsen*   ISBN: *1-59462-112-8*   **$19.95**
Henrik Ibsen created this classic when in revolutionary 1848 Rome. Introducing some striking concepts in playwriting for the realist genre, this play has been studied the world over.   Fiction/Classics/Plays 308

The Light of Asia *by sir Edwin Arnold*   ISBN: *1-59462-204-3*   **$13.95**
In this poetic masterpiece, Edwin Arnold describes the life and teachings of Buddha. The man who was to become known as Buddha to the world was born as Prince Gautama of India but he rejected the worldly riches and abandoned the reigns of power when...   Religion/History/Biographies Pages 170

The Complete Works of Guy de Maupassant *by Guy de Maupassant*   ISBN: *1-59462-157-8*   **$16.95**
"For days and days, nights and nights, I had dreamed of that first kiss which was to consecrate our engagement, and I knew not on what spot I should put my lips..."   Fiction/Classics Pages 240

The Art of Cross-Examination *by Francis L. Wellman*   ISBN: *1-59462-309-0*   **$26.95**
Written by a renowned trial lawyer, Wellman imparts his experience and uses case studies to explain how to use psychology to extract desired information through questioning.   How-to/Science/Reference Pages 408

Answered or Unanswered? *by Louisa Vaughan*   ISBN: *1-59462-248-5*   **$10.95**
Miracles of Faith in China   Religion Pages 112

The Edinburgh Lectures on Mental Science (1909) *by Thomas*   ISBN: *1-59462-008-5*   **$11.95**
This book contains the substance of a course of lectures recently given by the writer in the Queen Street Hall, Edinburgh. Its purpose is to indicate the Natural Principles governing the relation between Mental Action and Material Conditions...   New Age/Psychology Pages 148

Ayesha *by H. Rider Haggard*   ISBN: *1-59462-301-5*   **$24.95**
Verily and indeed it is the unexpected that happens! Probably if there was one person upon the earth from whom the Editor of this, and of a certain previous history, did not expect to hear again...   Classics Pages 380

Ayala's Angel *by Anthony Trollope*   ISBN: *1-59462-352-X*   **$29.95**
The two girls were both pretty, but Lucy who was twenty-one who supposed to be simple and comparatively unattractive, whereas Ayala was credited, as her Bombwhat romantic name might show, with poetic charm and a taste for romance. Ayala when her father died was nineteen...   Fiction Pages 484

The American Commonwealth *by James Bryce*   ISBN: *1-59462-286-8*   **$34.45**
An interpretation of American democratic political theory. It examines political mechanics and society from the perspective of Scotsman James Bryce   Politics Pages 572

Stories of the Pilgrims *by Margaret P. Pumphrey*   ISBN: *1-59462-116-0*   **$17.95**
This book explores pilgrims religious oppression in England as well as their escape to Holland and eventual crossing to America on the Mayflower, and their early days in New England...   History Pages 268

QTY

The Fasting Cure *by Sinclair Upton*   ISBN: *1-59462-222-1* **$13.95**
In the Cosmopolitan Magazine for May, 1910, and in the Contemporary Review (London) for April, 1910, I published an article dealing with my experi-
ences in fasting. I have written a great many magazine articles, but never one which attracted so much attention... New Age/Self Help/Health Pages 164

Hebrew Astrology *by Sepharial*   ISBN: *1-59462-308-2* **$13.45**
In these days of advanced thinking it is a matter of common observation that we have left many of the old landmarks behind and that we are now pressing
forward to greater heights and to a wider horizon than that which represented the mind-content of our progenitors...   Astrology Pages 144

Thought Vibration or The Law of Attraction in the Thought World   ISBN: *1-59462-127-6* **$12.95**

by William Walker Atkinson   *Psychology/Religion Pages 144*

Optimism *by Helen Keller*   ISBN: *1-59462-108-X* **$15.95**
Helen Keller was blind, deaf, and mute since 19 months old, yet famously learned how to overcome these handicaps, communicate with the world, and
spread her lectures promoting optimism. An inspiring read for everyone...   Biographies/Inspirational Pages 84

Sara Crewe *by Frances Burnett*   ISBN: *1-59462-360-0* **$9.45**
In the first place, Miss Minchin lived in London. Her home was a large, dull, tall one, in a large, dull square, where all the houses were alike, and all the
sparrows were alike, and where all the door-knockers made the same heavy sound...   Childrens/Classic Pages 88

The Autobiography of Benjamin Franklin *by Benjamin Franklin*   ISBN: *1-59462-135-7* **$24.95**
The Autobiography of Benjamin Franklin has probably been more extensively read than any other American historical work, and no other book of its kind
has had such ups and downs of fortune. Franklin lived for many years in England, where he was agent...   Biographies/History Pages 332

Name	
Email	
Telephone	
Address	
City, State ZIP	

☐ **Credit Card**   ☐ **Check / Money Order**

Credit Card Number	
Expiration Date	
Signature	

Please Mail to: Book Jungle
PO Box 2226
Champaign, IL 61825
or Fax to: 630-214-0564

ORDERING INFORMATION

web: *www.bookjungle.com*
email: *sales@bookjungle.com*
fax: *630-214-0564*
mail: *Book Jungle PO Box 2226 Champaign, IL 61825*
or PayPal *to sales@bookjungle.com*

Please contact us for bulk discounts

DIRECT-ORDER TERMS

**20% Discount if You Order
Two or More Books**
Free Domestic Shipping!
Accepted: Master Card, Visa,
Discover, American Express